DRACULA

FROM THE STORY BY BRAM STOKER

Retold by Mike Stocks
With introduction and notes by Anthony Marks
Illustrations by Barry Jones

First published in 2002 by Usborne Publishing Ltd,
Usborne House, 83-85 Saffron Hill, London
EC1N 8RT, England.
www.usborne.com

A catalogue record for this title is available from
the British Library

ISBN 07945 00897

Printed in Great Britain

Edited by Felicity Brooks & Anthony Marks
Designed by Brian Voakes
Series editors: Jane Chisholm & Rosie Dickins
Cover design by Amanda Gulliver & Steve Wright
Cover image by Barry Jones

❤ CONTENTS ❤

About Dracula

The author of *Dracula*, Bram Stoker, was born near Dublin, in Ireland, in 1847. He worked in the legal profession, then in the Irish civil service, and his first stories were published in the early 1870s. In 1877 he met Henry Irving, the most famous English actor of his day, when Irving gave a reading at Trinity College, Dublin. Shortly after this, Stoker moved with his wife to London and became Irving's theatrical manager, a position he held for 28 years. During this period he wrote many short stories and eleven novels, as well as his memoirs of his work with Irving.

But only one of these books remains well-known: *Dracula*. It is one of the most powerful horror stories of all time. Stoker began making notes for it in 1890 while visiting the North Yorkshire seaside town of Whitby, and it was eventually published in 1897. Since that date it has never been out of print. It has also been translated into nearly fifty languages. Count Dracula remains one of the most popular figures in contemporary horror fiction, represented in countless films, books and comics.

Dracula draws its inspiration from many sources. Its

dark, brooding style, and episodes of bloodthirsty terror, resemble the horror and suspense stories (known as Gothic novels) that became popular in the previous century, with books like Walpole's *The Castle of Otranto* and Anne Radcliffe's *The Mysteries of Udolpho*. Tales of blood-sucking monsters can be found in various ancient civilizations, including China, Greece and the Babylonian and Assyrian empires. Medieval vampire legends were common in such Eastern European countries as Albania, Hungary and Romania, and vampire stories had already been served up to British readers in the form of works like Polidori's *The Vampyre* (1819) and the anonymous *Varney the Vampire* (1846).

There were also several historical characters that Stoker may have been familiar with. These included a 16th-century Eastern European count, Vlad Tepes (Vlad the Impaler), who was also known as *dracul*, the local word for "devil", and the Blood Countess, a 16th-century Hungarian aristocrat who liked to bathe in the blood of animals and young women, because she believed it would keep her young. All these elements combine in Stoker's book to create a dramatic portrayal of evil.

But *Dracula* was far more successful than other vampire novels before or since. There are two main reasons for this. Firstly, from the middle of the 18th century, people had been taught that science, reason, industry and wealth would solve the world's problems. But during the Victorian era, many people began to doubt this, feeling that industry and technology had created the horrors of inner city slums and that science and wealth had failed to eradicate disease and decay. *Dracula* tapped into these fears by including a scientist, a lawyer and an aristocrat in the group of people who are challenged to conquer the vampire. It is noticeable that up-to-date medical knowledge cannot help them (for example, blood transfusions do not help Lucy). Instead they have to rely on Dr. Van Helsing's obscure library research, and on other more traditional values, such as the physical strength of Jonathan Harker and Arthur Holmwood, and on Mina Harker's bravery.

Secondly, by beginning his novel with Harker's visit to the vampire's castle in Transylvania, Stoker drew readers in by appealing to their appetite for exotic places. The Victorian era saw a huge growth in foreign travel, as well as a boom in travel writing. But he did not allow the terror to remain a distant fantasy. Instead he brought the vampire to England and eventually to the heart of London, placing unimaginable evil right on the doorsteps of his readers. While most earlier horror tales were set in the past, or in remote places, much of the action of *Dracula* happened in the Victorian reader's own time and place. And though the world has changed since the book was written, our fears have not – which is why *Dracula* remains a classic.

Castle Dracula

It was the dead of night. Jonathan Harker sat bolt upright in bed and screamed "No-oooo!" His brow was covered in sweat, his heart beat furiously, and he was so scared that he didn't know where he was. Then, slowly, it all came back to him – he was at an inn in Transylvania, one of the wildest, least-known parts of Europe. "What a creepy dream," he thought. "Those horrible wolves. And that huge bat which wrapped its wings around me. . ." He shuddered.

Next morning he received a letter.

My dear friend,

Welcome to Transylvania. I am particularly looking forward to meeting you in the flesh.

I have arranged for you to travel by the afternoon stagecoach to the Borgo Pass, where my carriage will bring you to my castle.

Count Dracula

As Jonathan was getting ready to leave, the landlady surprised him by coming to his room, and pleading desperately with him not to go.

"But it's my job as a lawyer," he explained, feeling slightly embarrassed. "I've organized all the legal details of the Count's new house in London, and I need to explain to him how. . . Oh! Please don't be upset."

"Tonight," whispered the old lady, "all the evil in the world will be let loose. You will be at the mercy of forces you never dreamed existed. You must not go!"

"Did you have nightmares as well?" Jonathan joked, trying to make light of the situation. "I did. First this gigantic bat wrapped its slimy wings around me, then as I screamed in terror it sank its teeth into my. . . Are you alright?"

The old lady was moaning and gasping in horror, making him regret being so flippant. So when she held out in her hand a chain with a cross on it, he looked at her solemnly.

"For the sake of your soul," she begged, "always wear this crucifix."

"I will," he said in a quiet voice.

When the other passengers on the stagecoach found out where Jonathan was going, they stared at him in astonishment. Then they started whispering in Transylvanian and Jonathan heard some words that he knew: *pokol* and *vrolok*. The first word meant hell, and the second. . . Jonathan shivered. It meant vampire. But he told himself that such fears were merely absurd superstitions. When he met the Count, it would be interesting to discuss them.

Even though the roads were rough, winding and dangerous, the driver seemed to be in a frantic hurry. Jonathan watched the countryside flash past, a landscape of steep hills, green forests and sudden spectacular views of craggy mountains. When it started to get dark, the driver urged his horses to go even faster, and the stagecoach swayed and rocked like a boat on a stormy sea. They entered the Borgo Pass at a full gallop, then the driver pulled hard on the reins and the carriage lurched to a halt. Jonathan was glad they had arrived — the other passengers were starting to get on his nerves. Half the time they were whispering that his soul was in eternal peril, and the rest of the time they kept trying to press cloves of garlic into his hand. Why? thought Jonathan, as he secretly dropped yet another clove out of the window.

"This is the Borgo Pass, but there's no carriage waiting for you," said the driver with a great sigh of relief. "You're not expected after all." It was a cold night, but there were beads of sweat on his face. "We'll drive on, as fast as we can, and you can return tomorrow — and with a different driver, too," he added in a low voice.

But before he had finished speaking, his horses began to snort and stamp wildly, and out of the surrounding darkness a four-horse carriage thundered up to them. When they saw the tall, dark driver, the other passengers screamed and cowered. His face was obscured by a long, brown beard, and a large, black hat. But nothing could obscure the fact that his eyes flashed red in the blackness of the night.

"The stagecoach has never been so early," he observed, smiling from a cruel-looking mouth, his voice harsh and malevolent. "Now," he commanded, "the English gentleman will come with me."

Jonathan's fellow passengers suddenly seemed like the most cheerful, friendly and fascinating bunch of people he had ever met. There was nothing he wanted less than to leave them and go with the tall, dark man. But he felt that he had no choice, so he got out of the stagecoach and collected his luggage from the roof. His anxiety was not eased when the door of the carriage flew open of its own accord, trembling on its hinges. And when he got in, the door slammed shut behind him so hard that the noise echoed across the mountains, like nails being banged into a coffin. Then, before he could even sit down, the carriage surged forward and swept him away into the night.

The journey took hours. They rose ever higher up the perilous paths of the thickly forested mountains, the driver savagely cracking his whip as the horses struggled to climb the steep slopes. Bats flitted above them in great numbers, and by the edge of the road there were hundreds of wooden crosses which, Jonathan suddenly realized with horror, were graves. Everything was so creepy that he wished he had stayed in England. He thought about his fiancée, Mina. She would be at home now, marking her pupils' homework, or perhaps sitting snugly in front of a log fire, eating hot, buttered toast.

Then, finally, the trip drew to a close. They journeyed along a track to a vast, forbidding castle, as wolves bayed malevolently into the darkness of the night. When they arrived, and Jonathan was left alone in the courtyard, he could see the castle's broken battlements etched against a moonlit sky. Not a ray of light came from the high, black windows. Directly in front of him was a huge, wooden door, and beyond it he heard heavy steps approaching: clump, clump, clump. There was a rattling of chains and a clanking of bolts. Then very slowly, the old door creaked open.

A tall, old man was standing in the doorway, dressed from head to foot in black. He had a sneering mouth with two sharp white teeth protruding over his lips.

"Welcome to my house!" he said, and then, almost eagerly, "Won't you come inside?"

Jonathan winced when he shook hands with him. The old man's grip was like a steel trap, and his hand was as cold as ice, like the hand of a dead man. And there was something else very curious about it: the palm was covered in hair.

11

"Count Dracula?" Jonathan asked nervously.

"I am Dracula," the old man replied in a chilling voice, "and I welcome you, Mr. Harker."

The Count bowed to Jonathan, who felt a sudden shudder. Perhaps it was just that the Count's breath was revolting, but there was something about the man that was making him feel sick.

The freezing stone corridors they walked along did nothing to raise Jonathan's spirits. Nor did the narrow staircases, the damp walls, or the heavy bolted doors. But at last the Count led him to a comfortable study. A fire was burning in the hearth, and an open door revealed an adjoining bedroom. Suddenly Jonathan felt much better. To see a warm fire was comforting, and his welcome to Castle Dracula had at least been. . . well, polite. After all, it wasn't the Count's fault if he had hair on the palms of his hands, or breath so bad that it could fell an ox.

"You must be hungry after your journey," the Count said, pointing to a table where a substantial meal was laid out. "You will excuse me if I do not join you. My eating habits are rather. . . er, unconventional."

Neither of them spoke much as Jonathan was eating, but when he had finished, the Count said, "And now, my friend, tell me all about my new house in London." So Jonathan got the property deeds out from his luggage. Clause by clause, he explained the numerous legal arrangements. Then he asked the Count to sign various papers and documents.

"But is the house exactly as I requested?" the Count asked.

"Oh yes," said Jonathan, who had seen the place with his own eyes. He wondered why anyone would want to buy such a crumbling old dump. Carfax was dark and damp and gloomy. It was falling to pieces. It was next door to a lunatic asylum. "The property is a most desirable residence," said Jonathan.

Count Dracula kept Jonathan talking about England, and London in particular, for so long that it was nearly dawn when he left.

"Lie in as long as you like tomorrow," he said gravely, pausing in the doorway. "I have important affairs to attend to until evening. Sleep well, Mr. Harker. . ."

Before finally going to bed, Jonathan sat down at a desk and described the day's events in his journal. It was a diary of all his Transylvanian experiences which he was keeping for Mina. He smiled as he wrote, imagining her reading it. She would laugh her head off at how nervous he had been earlier.

He woke up so late the next day that it was already dark. He couldn't find a mirror in his bedroom, so he hung up his own shaving-mirror by the window. As he slowly dragged the razor across his chin by the light of a lamp, he idly wondered why there was no mirror.

"Good day," said the Count's voice, from nowhere. Jonathan jumped in surprise, cutting himself with the blade. He blurted out a gabbled greeting, then turned back to the mirror. A cold feeling suddenly swept over him. He could see his own reflection, a glistening trickle of blood running down his chin. And behind his face he could see the rest of the room. But he couldn't see the Count.

He turned around again, very, very slowly. It was inexplicable – there was the Count, as large as life, standing right behind him. . . and he was staring at the blood on Jonathan's chin. The Count's nose began to twitch, and he licked his lips. Then, as quick as lightning, his hand shot out and made a grab for Jonathan's throat. Jonathan stepped back in alarm, and the Count's hand touched the chain of the crucifix. In an instant the old man regained control over himself.

"Take care," he warned in a strange voice, breathing heavily. "Take care not to cut yourself in this place. It could be dangerous." Then he seized the mirror. "This wretched object has caused all the trouble – away with it!" And he crushed it to smithereens in his bare hands, and furiously flung it out of the window.

There was a meal waiting for Jonathan in the study. He picked at it listlessly, alone and very afraid. After throwing the mirror away, the Count had left, without a word of explanation. Jonathan wrote about the incident in his journal. Then, as the Count didn't seem to be around, he decided to explore the castle. Taking a lamp with him, he set off.

It was cold in the echoing stone corridors. He hurried along them, trying out doors on each side. He noticed that there was thick dust on the handles, as though no one had used them for years. Each one he tried seemed to be locked. But it was a big place, so he made his way to another floor. There were hundreds more doors to try. One of them was bound to be open. He grabbed another handle. Locked. Jonathan tried to ignore the sinking feeling in his stomach.

After another hour, he knew the dreadful truth: he was a prisoner. He sat down on the top step of a stone staircase, and closed his eyes. For some minutes he sat motionless, listening to his own heartbeat.

On the way back to his room Jonathan noticed that one of the locked doors was rotten. Soon he would wish that he had never laid eyes on that door, or witnessed what lay beyond it. But now his spirits lifted. He pushed and kicked at it, and shouted in triumph when it burst open. With his head full of thoughts of escape, he went through the doorway.

He found himself in a luxurious suite of rooms, with walls of dark wood panels, filled with exquisite antique furniture and paintings. Thick dust covered everything, and enormous cobwebs were suspended from every corner. The silence of centuries hung in the air. Jonathan sat down on a soft, velvet-covered couch. For some reason he was starting to feel very sleepy. It was almost as if there were some strange force in the room – a force which was impossible to resist. He lay back on the couch, and went into a sort of trance.

It felt like a dream when three young women approached through the moonlight. Two were dark, with piercing eyes that seemed to flash red. The other was fair, with masses of wavy golden hair and eyes like sapphires. All three had brilliant white teeth, which shone like pearls against the deep red of their lips. They were very beautiful.

"You go first," said one of them. "He's young and strong, and there's enough blood for us all."

The fair girl bent over him. Jonathan watched her from under his eyelashes. He couldn't move. He could only look on in fascination. She was staring at his neck. She licked her lips, like a hungry animal. Then he felt two sharp points against his throat, pressing on the skin. Hopelessly, helplessly, Jonathan waited.

"Get back!" a voice roared from somewhere, waking Jonathan from his trance and plunging him into terror. He tried to shrink away from the sharp teeth which were just about to puncture his skin. As he did so he saw Count Dracula's hairy hand grip the girl's shoulder. The Count pulled her away with the strength of a giant, and she shot across the room. His eyes were on fire, his face was chalk-white, and his voice cut through the air like a deadly blade.

"He's mine!" he hissed.

"Are we to have nothing tonight?" one of the demon women whined.

"Before two nights have passed," said Dracula chillingly, "it will be time for him to die, and he will be yours. But do not meddle with him until I say. Now go!"

In front of Jonathan's eyes, the three women began to fade in the rays of moonlight. Before they disappeared into a million specks and seeped out of the window, he saw the fair one smiling at him and heard her low, sweet ripple of laughter. Then horror overcame him, and he sank down into unconsciousness.

Jonathan awoke in his own bed in his room. He noticed that his clothes were folded in a neat pile on a chair, as though someone had put him to bed. Then he remembered what had happened, how those dreadful women had been ready to drink him dry of blood, and he covered his face with his hands.

Later that day there was a great commotion in the courtyard. Jonathan looked out of the window. Below there was a band of gypsies with two great wagons, each loaded with large boxes and drawn by eight sturdy horses. The boxes were obviously empty, because the gypsies were unloading them with ease and stacking them in a corner. Jonathan leaned out of the window.

"Help me!" he cried. "I'm a prisoner! Please help me!"

But the gypsies just pointed at him and started to laugh. They were still laughing later, when their empty wagons rumbled out of the cobbled courtyard.

Jonathan had noticed that he never saw the Count in the daytime. Was it possible that he was sleeping when others were awake, and awake when others were sleeping? He decided that when the morning came he would try to find the Count's room. He knew it was a desperate, hopeless act, but he was in a desperate, hopeless situation, and it would be better to die bravely than wait to have the blood sucked out of him by those vampires.

When the sun rose over Castle Dracula early the next day, it revealed Jonathan, perching precariously on the narrow ledge outside his bedroom window, trying not to look down at the sheer drop below. He felt his heart pounding as his hands groped for holds in the rock of the castle wall. Perilously, inch by inch,

he began his slow
descent.

He re-entered
the castle by a small
arched window far
below, and found
himself at the top of
a narrow spiral
staircase. After he had
got his breath back he
went down it, farther and
farther, as if descending
into hell itself. Eventually he
came to the bottom, where he found
himself in an old ruined chapel.

Jonathan wrinkled his nose in disgust. The place
was dirty and dank, and every so often he could hear
the sound of scuttling rats. Cautiously, he made his
way deeper and deeper into the chapel. As he did so,
he noticed a peculiar smell. It baffled him at first, but
after a while he realized what it was: the smell of
freshly dug soil. It was coming from the far end of the
chapel, where there were lots of boxes – the boxes
that he had seen the gypsies unloading in the
courtyard. He made a quick investigation. There
were about forty-five of them, maybe more. Each
one was half-filled with soil.

Walking around them, he came across a low
doorway in the wall. Hesitantly he pushed his head
through the opening, feeling terrified about what

might be inside. It seemed to be some kind of vault, a chamber in the ground used for burials.

The interior was dimly lit by sputtering candles. Jonathan wiped his brow, which was damp with sweat, before stepping inside and. . .

"Aaah!" he shouted suddenly, stepping back in panic as something brushed against his face.

It was only a cobweb, but it startled him so much that his breath came in great, heaving gasps. He tried to calm down, telling himself not to be scared. After all, he reflected as he went farther into the vault, it's only natural for a damp and dingy place like this to be full of cobwebs, not to mention. . .

"Waah!" he yelled, as an enormous rat ran over his feet, squeaking horribly.

Again he stopped, desperately trying to calm himself down. But now it was perfectly obvious to him that he was in a foul and evil place, a place where something terrible was waiting to happen. Even the smell in the air was vile and terrifying, like the Count's breath, only worse.

Finally, in the very heart of the vault, he found a last box. This one had a lid on it. Jonathan placed his lamp on a ledge and grasped the lid. In his heart he already knew what was inside, but he hardly dared admit it. . . Slowly, as shadows flickered over the walls, he began to lift.

There was a loud creak. He opened it wider, then suddenly had to put his free hand over his nose, spluttering and coughing as an indescribable stench of death and evil seeped out of the box. And there, lying on a great mound of earth, neither asleep nor dead, was Dracula!

His white hair was now dark grey. His cheeks were fuller and less pale, and his face was less wrinkled. And on his lips was fresh blood, trickling bright red from the corners of his mouth and down over his chin and neck. It seemed as if the hideous creature was simply gorged with blood, blood which had renewed his youth, for he looked at least twenty years younger. He lay, like a filthy leech, bursting with all the horrible crimes he had ever committed.

Jonathan shook all over. He couldn't help it. This confirmed his worst suspicions: the terrible realization that the ghoulish Count was indeed a vampire. To think that this horrible creature was heading for London where – perhaps for centuries – he might prey on innocent people and suck their blood. The idea drove Jonathan almost insane with fury. Seizing a shovel which lay on the ground nearby, he lifted it up high and, with all his strength, brought it down swiftly on the vampire's face.

Dracula's veiny hand shot out to fend off the blow, and his red eyes opened, rolling horribly to stare at his assailant. Jonathan felt the shovel spin around in his grip, as though an invisible force had taken control of it, and the blade smashed harmlessly into the side of the box. Then the vampire's eyes closed once more, and the lid slammed shut with an echoing crash. Jonathan's final glimpse was of a bloated, bloodstained face, its mouth set into a malicious grin.

As he stepped back, trying to overcome the urge to run away, the shovel fell from his hands. Taking a deep breath, he picked it up again and grasped the lid of the box. His instinct for survival told him that he had to kill Dracula! But just as he began to raise the lid a second time, he heard something – footsteps, shouts, orders, and people running towards him. It sounded like the gypsies. They were very near and getting nearer. Jonathan cursed silently, running quickly out of the vault and the chapel, and up the spiral stairs. In despair, he made the long, exhausting journey back to his own room. He collapsed in a heap by the old window and looked out at the jagged, rocky mountain ranges of Transylvania. For as long as he lived (which didn't look as if it was going to be very long) he would never, ever forget the loathsome expression on Dracula's bloodstained face.

In the courtyard below, the gypsies were starting to load the boxes of earth onto their wagons. Jonathan knew that the containers were going to England, and one of them had Dracula in it. He clenched his fists in powerless anger and grief.

Back in his room, Jonathan spent the night wide awake, petrified of what was going to happen to him, and jumping in fright at even the tiniest sound. He feverishly scribbled in his journal:

I'm all alone. I've never felt so desolate in my life, knowing that I've been left here as a . . . as a slap-up feast for those three things — monsters — vampires! I must escape!
I'll climb down the walls again to the very bottom and take my chances with the wolves in the forest. I'd rather die out there than in here. Mina, it breaks my heart to think that I'll never see you again.
Goodbye, Mina . . . goodbye . . .

Then there was a sound which froze his blood. He stood up, knocking his chair to the floor, and listened in terror. From outside his door came a noise he had heard once before. It was a low, sweet ripple of laughter. The laughter of the vampires.

The Ship with No Crew

In England a month later, Mina, Jonathan's fiancée, sent a letter to her friend Lucy Westenra in the seaside town of Whitby in Yorkshire. Mina had been Lucy's teacher a few years earlier, but now that Lucy was older they had become as close as sisters.

Dearest Lucy,

Thank goodness the school term ends this week. I'm worn out, and I'm so worried about Jonathan. I still haven't heard from him. But coming to Whitby to stay with you will cheer me up. We can sit on the old seat we always sit on, by the graveyard on the cliff top, and talk about all our news. Speaking of which, is it true that you have become engaged to a certain Arthur Holmwood? You can tell me all about it when I see you in a few days.

Much love,
Mina xxx

P.S. Your mother told me that in the last few nights you have started sleepwalking. It sounds mysterious. I shall have to keep a close eye on you!

A storm was brewing out at sea when Mina arrived in Whitby. Sitting on the clifftop seat with Lucy in the evening, Mina watched the swelling waves. All the fishing boats were making for port as fast as they could sail, and the sky was getting blacker every moment. Even the air around them seemed heavy and oppressive. It made Mina feel nervous, as though something unpleasant was about to happen.

"So Arthur got down on one knee and proposed," Lucy was saying, ". . . and I said, 'Arthur, I'm so happy I could *faint*,' and he said. . ."

Mina had heard this story already: once before breakfast, twice during breakfast, three times after breakfast, and about a million times since. It was beginning to get on her nerves.

"I think we'd better go home now," Mina said.

". . . and he said, 'I love you so much that sometimes I think my head's just going to *fall off*,' " Lucy continued in a dreamy voice as she stood up and collected all her things together.

"Look at that ship," Mina said, pointing far out to sea at a large schooner. "It doesn't seem to be making any attempt to get to shore." Still musing dreamily about Arthur, Lucy looked up. When she saw the ship, she stopped talking in mid-sentence, and her face went pale. A look of melancholy filled her eyes.

"Lucy? What's the matter? Are you all right?"

"I think so," Lucy said, quietly. "It's that ship. I just looked at it, and I felt. . . odd."

"I'll take you home," Mina said, holding her by the arm.

It was the worst storm since records began, and it blew up in minutes. The waves rose in fury, each one bigger and angrier than the last, before crashing onto the beach and lashing the cliffs. The wind roared as loud as thunder, and great flashes of lightning cracked like enormous whips in the sky, revealing black clouds gathered like huge rocks waiting to fall.

On the summit of Whitby's West Cliff, the local coastguard trained a searchlight out to sea in case there were still any boats out there. Around him there was an excited crowd of townspeople who had come to observe the grandeur and fury of the storm. The searchlight soon picked out the lone schooner, and everyone pointed and shouted into the gale.

The ship had all sails set, and the wind was driving it to the shore at ferocious speed. But between the schooner and safety lay a flat reef on which many a ship had been wrecked. It didn't seem possible that she could avoid it. Then fierce winds swept in more huge clouds of seafog, and for some moments nothing could be seen. The coastguard's searchlight was of no use. The crowd waited, motionless, and wondered if they would be able to hear the doomed ship splintering into pieces above the crash and roar of the storm.

But when the fog passed, they were amazed to see that the schooner had somehow found a narrow gap in the deadly reef. The ship was now leaping from wave to wave at headlong speed. It was being blown straight to the safety of the shore!

The townspeople cheered with relief, jumping up and down in joy; and yet, within a few moments, the cheering had turned into a collective gasp of horror. The coastguard had managed to train his searchlight on the schooner again, revealing a sight so gruesome that it made people hold on to each other in terror.

Lashed to the wheel of the ship, swinging horribly to and fro as the vessel was battered by the waves, was a dead man. No one else could be seen on board. The ship had reached the safety of the shore steered by a corpse.

The watching crowd barely had time to take this in before the ship ran aground. Every timber strained and shuddered as it slammed into the beach, and two of its masts crashed to the deck. But the strangest thing of all was the immense dog which appeared from below deck and, with a huge leap, jumped from the ship to land. Its eyes blazing red, it made straight for the East Cliff, where the graveyard of the parish church was crumbling into the sea.

It was a restless night for Mina as the storm raged. Twice she had woken and found Lucy sleepwalking, looking out of the window at the tempest of the sea. Each time Mina had led her gently back to her bed. They both slept very late into the morning. When they finally got up and went down to breakfast, Mrs. Westenra, Lucy's mother, was waiting for them. She had heard all about the mysterious schooner, and she was impatient to tell them about it.

"What a terrible tragedy," Mina whispered, when Mrs. Westenra had finished her breathless tale. "What did the dead captain look like?" Lucy asked.

Mrs. Westenra had no idea, but that wasn't going to stop her.

"He was a very handsome young fellow," she asserted, "with a good strong face, and jet-black hair."

"It's very strange indeed about the dog," Mina said. "I wonder what sort it was."

"It was an enormous dog," claimed Mrs. Westenra, who knew even less about the dog than she knew about the captain, "the biggest dog ever, bigger than a horse, bigger than an elephant. . ."

"Mother!" said Lucy, laughing.

"Well, as big as a really big dog," Mrs. Westenra conceded, "with huge, evil, bright-red eyes. They say it had two heads and six legs, and. . ."

"*Two* heads?" Lucy asked.

"*Six* legs?" Mina queried.

"Or possibly one head," Mrs. Westenra admitted, "and about four legs at the most, but that's not the point. The point is, it was the scariest, deadliest, most evil beast I ever laid eyes on."

"Oh, so you actually saw the animal?" Mina asked.

"Um. . ." said Mrs. Westenra, dabbing at her lips with a napkin, "more tea dear?"

Mina was incredibly disappointed that no letter arrived from Jonathan that day. No letter arrived on the following day either, nor the day after that. She couldn't imagine why he hadn't written, and began to wonder if something had happened to him. It became difficult to stay cheerful as the days passed with no news. And Lucy's sleepwalking was getting worse, which was also very worrying. In fact ever since that dreadful night of the storm, when a foreign ship steered by a dead man had mysteriously delivered a huge dog to Whitby, it was as though the whole town was on edge. The local newspaper was reporting more and more bizarre details about the story, and every morning Mrs. Westenra would gossip about it.

"The ship had a cargo of fifty boxes," she told them, squinting through her reading glasses at *The Whitby Times,* "all addressed to a secret location in London, and each one full to the brim with something terrible."

"What do you mean, *terrible?*" asked Lucy, reaching for another piece of toast.

"Well it says here that they were just filled with soil," murmured Mrs. Westenra in a low voice, "but, you see, I know what was *really* in them."

"And what was that?"

Mrs. Westenra frowned, deep in thought. She tried hard to think of something thrillingly scary. Unfortunately she couldn't think of anything, so she quickly changed the subject.

"And as for the Captain's logbook," she said, "well you don't want to hear about it. You aren't old enough to hear what was in that logbook. If I told you what was in that logbook, you'd never sleep a wink at night. I wouldn't tell you what was recorded in that logbook," she claimed, looking slowly from one to the other, and then slowly back again, "even if you *begged* me."

"So what was recorded in the logbook?" asked Lucy in a bored voice.

"All the crew were horribly murdered one by one by an evil presence," gabbled her mother breathlessly. "The captain had the ship searched time and again but never found anything. Eventually he was the only one left. And when the authorities untied him from the wheel of that ship, they discovered that he was holding a crucifix – to protect himself against *it*."

"Oh," said Lucy quietly, her eyes filling with tears. "How awful. He must have been so terrified. I wish you hadn't told me that."

"You shouldn't have dragged it from me," her mother said.

One night, Mina woke up abruptly with the distinct feeling that something was very wrong.

"Lucy?" she called.

There was no reply from Lucy's bed. Mina struck a match and lit a candle. The pale, quivering flame revealed that her friend's bed was empty. Mina searched the upstairs rooms before going downstairs.

In the hall her heart sank. The front door was open – Lucy had gone outside. It was a cold night, and Mina knew that her friend was wearing just a thin nightdress. Hurriedly throwing a shawl around her own shoulders, she went to look for her.

The church clock was striking one as Mina ran through the streets of Whitby. She kept a sharp lookout, but there was no sign of the white figure she had expected to see. She ran along the Crescent, then she explored along the North Terrace – nothing. Searching farther and farther away from the house, she made her way up to the West Cliff.

At the edge of the West Cliff she looked across the bay to the East Cliff. There was a bright full moon but also lots of swift-moving clouds, so a dappled light was moving across the sea and the town. For some time she couldn't distinguish very much at all. Then the moon emerged fully, casting a narrow strip of cold blue light over the East Cliff.

Mina could see the tombstones of the old graveyard, leaning over at crazy angles, making dark silhouettes against the wild night sky. The strip of light moved steadily along the tombstones and memorials. And there on their seat, was the half-reclining, snowy-white figure of Lucy.

Almost as soon as she spotted her friend, the moon went in. But it seemed to Mina that something dark had been standing behind Lucy, or leaning over her. Whether it was man or beast Mina wasn't sure.

She started running down the slope of the West

Cliff as fast as she could. It seemed to take forever. Eventually she was leaping up the endless steps of the East Cliff, her legs shaky with tiredness. As she neared the graveyard on the cliff top she gasped. She had been right. A dark shape was leaning over her friend.

"Lucy! Lucy!" she called in fright.

At the sound of her voice, the dark figure raised its head. Mina saw a pale face and red, gleaming eyes. For a moment they flashed at her. Then, as Mina got closer, the dark figure seemed to melt into the surrounding blackness.

"Lucy!" Mina cried, throwing herself next to her friend on the bench.

Lucy was still asleep. Her lips were parted, and she was breathing in long, heavy gasps. She put her hand to her throat and moaned. Mina wrapped her shawl around her friend's shoulders. Lucy seemed unusually cold and gave a shudder. Using a safety pin, Mina fastened the shawl at Lucy's throat. But she must have been clumsy, because Lucy's hands went to her throat again, and Mina noticed that there were two little red marks on her neck. Mina thought that she must have pricked her accidentally.

"Wake up, Lucy" she whispered, shaking her gently. "Wake up!"

Lucy's eyes opened and looked at Mina with wonder. She didn't seem to understand where she was. She started to tremble, and clung to her friend.

"We must walk home," Mina said softly.

She pulled Lucy to her feet, and putting an arm around her shoulder, began to walk her home. When they got there, Lucy begged Mina not to tell Mrs. Westenra anything of what had happened. Her mother's health was already poor, and Lucy didn't want to make things worse by worrying her.

Mina locked their door from the inside and tied the key to her wrist. She put Lucy to bed, and, once she was asleep, got into bed herself. But she couldn't stop thinking about what had happened. Who – or what – was that dark figure she had seen leaning over Lucy? When at last she finally fell asleep, she dreamed that Lucy was sleepwalking again, rattling the handle of the bedroom door. The door didn't open, so Lucy moved to the window and pointed outside: a great bat was flitting through the moonlight, coming and going in whirling circles. It was such a vivid dream that it felt real.

"Letters for you both today," said Mrs. Westenra in the morning.

Mina and Lucy ripped open their envelopes.

"Are you all right, Lucy?" Mrs. Westenra asked. "You look a little ill this morning, rather pale –

almost as if you didn't have enough blood in your veins!" she joked.

"I'm fine," Lucy said. "Listen to this, mother – Arthur says he's sorry, but he definitely can't come to Whitby because his father is ill, so he wants us to go back to our house in London. He wants the wedding to be arranged as quickly as possible!"

"Well that's very good news, dear," said Mrs. Westenra. "And you, Mina? Any news of Jonathan?"

"Yes," said Mina after a long pause, scanning her letter with great concentration.

"I suppose it must be a private letter, then?" Mrs. Westenra speculated.

"Yes," Mina agreed, after an equally long pause.

"Well don't go telling me what it says, dear," Mrs. Westenra said. "Other people's private letters don't interest me in the slightest."

Mrs. Westenra saw Mina's eyes widen with shock.

"Is it a very interesting letter?" she couldn't help asking.

But Mina just kept on reading.

"Not that I want to know what it's about," Mrs. Westenra emphasized. "I wouldn't let you tell me even if you wanted to. I don't find interesting letters particularly. . . interesting," she claimed feebly.

"I'm just going to my room," Mina said in a strange voice, "to read my letter again."

"Shall I come too dear?" Mrs. Westenra asked, hastily standing up and knocking over the sugar bowl as she did so.

In the bedroom Mina shut the door firmly, took a deep breath, and carefully read the letter again.

Dear Madam,

I am writing on behalf of Mr. Jonathan Harker, who is not strong enough to write himself. He has been in our hospital for two months suffering from a violent brain fever. He has had some sort of terrible shock. He raves of wolves and blood, of monsters and demons. He came to us in the middle of the night, from where we do not know. He is mentally and physically exhausted, but getting better slowly but surely. Only recently was he able to say who he was, and who we should write to. He talks about you in his sleep. I can assure you that he will receive the very best care until he is ready to return home. I wish you both many happy years together.

Sister Agatha
St. Joseph Hospital, Budapest

Mina didn't know whether to cry with sorrow or laugh with relief. She knew there was only one thing to do. She threw open the cupboard doors, pulled her suitcase out, and began to pack.

Horror at Hillingham

It was a long and exhausting journey to Budapest, but when Mina arrived she went straight to the hospital. Sister Agatha led her to Jonathan's room.

"Try not to show any surprise at the way he looks," she whispered outside the door.

"Of course not," said Mina.

"His dreams and ravings have been so dreadful that no one can imagine what he has been through."

Sister Agatha opened the door and they entered. Despite Sister Agatha's warning, Mina gasped when she saw Jonathan. She couldn't help it. He was so pitifully weak and thin, his eyes staring hugely from his pale, gaunt face.

"Jonathan!"

"Mina!"

"Jonathan, what happened to you?" Mina cried, hugging him.

Jonathan pulled away from her and put his head in his hands, struggling to overcome his emotions.

"I've had a. . . a terrible shock," he whispered. "A great shock. I never thought I'd see you again. When I think of what I've seen. . . the terror of. . . and. . . his red eyes. . . Oh Mina! I don't know if it was real or if I'm mad!"

"Tell me about it," said Mina.

Jonathan shook his head. He reached under his pillow and pulled out his journal.

"It's all in this book, Mina.

You take it. Read it if you have to. I can't. I never want to read a word of it in case. . ."

"In case what?"

"In case it is true!" Jonathan cried in anguish.

Mina stayed silent for a few moments, trying to decide on the best course of action.

"Jonathan, I don't want us to live in the past. I'll put this book somewhere safe, but I'll never read it unless it's absolutely necessary." She took his hand in hers. "The most important thing is that you get your health back. I want us to be happy, Jonathan. Happy and strong, like Lucy and Arthur."

But back in England at that very moment, Arthur was pacing up and down outside Lucy's room. He was worried sick about her. Ever since returning from her holiday in Whitby to Hillingham, her family home in London, her health had steadily declined. Arthur had asked his friend Jack Seward to look at her. Jack was renowned for his expertise in psychiatry, running a large mental hospital on the outskirts of London; but he was also an experienced medical doctor.

"What's taking him so long?" Arthur muttered to himself as he waited in the corridor.

Then his friend came out of Lucy's room, closing the door gently behind him. He paused before speaking. Jack was a dark, brooding, melancholic man, and this had been no easy task for him. He too had once been in love with Lucy, and had even proposed to her.

"Well?" Arthur said. "Did you examine her?"

"Yes I did," said Jack, nodding.

"And have you come to any conclusion?"

"Yes I have," Jack answered solemnly. There was a silence which Jack showed no sign of breaking.

"Well, tell me, what is your conclusion?" Arthur implored him.

"The conclusion I have come to," said Jack, gravely, "and listen to this very carefully indeed, Arthur, as it's most important –"

"Yes, yes, get on with it," Arthur said impatiently.

"The conclusion I have come to, after a detailed, extensive examination of the patient, during which I employed the very latest techniques available to modern medical science, is that I have absolutely no idea what's wrong with her."

Arthur stared at him.

"But you're a fully qualified doctor!" he exploded.

"She complains of being tired all the time," Jack said, almost to himself. "And sometimes she has difficulty in breathing. She has bad dreams, and irrational fears — bats, wolves, things like that. She looks far too pale, which suggests a blood disorder or an iron deficiency, for example. I tested for them and found nothing. But nevertheless. . ."

He fell into a deep silence.

After what seemed like an age, Arthur could bear the silence no longer.

"But nevertheless *what*?" he implored.

"It's something to do with her blood, I'm sure."

"So what are you going to do, Jack? Do you know?"

"Yes. I'm absolutely clear about that. It's obvious. There's only one thing I can do."

"And what's that?"

"Nothing."

"Nothing!" Arthur shouted, hitting the wall blindly in frustration.

"As I don't know what to do, I'm going to do nothing," Jack said, shaking his head sadly. It seemed perfectly logical to him, and he couldn't understand why Arthur was being so unreasonable about it. "Clearly," he went on, "the patient must be examined by Professor Van Helsing."

"Professor Van Helsing?" Arthur repeated, watching as Jack began to stride along the corridor to the stairs. "I've never heard of Professor Van Helsing. Who on earth is this Professor Van Helsing person?"

"Professor Van Helsing is a distinguished doctor and scientist," Jack replied, taking the steps three at a time. "If anyone will know what's wrong with Lucy, he will."

Professor Van Helsing lived in Holland. Although he could be rather absent-minded and eccentric, he had devoted his life to science, and he knew more about obscure diseases than any living person. He taught at the Amsterdam School of Medicine, which is where Jack had met him. Jack had been his best, most brilliant pupil.

As soon as the Professor received Jack's telegram about Lucy's strange illness, he abandoned all his work and started packing. He didn't like the sound of her symptoms at all, so he completed the journey as fast as possible. Arthur and Jack were waiting for him when he arrived the next evening.

"Good morning to you, Jack!" the Professor called cheerfully.

"Good evening, Professor Van Helsing," replied Jack, smiling.

"Is it evening already?" the Professor asked.

"Yes. Morning was – well, earlier," Jack explained.

"Just before lunch," Arthur helpfully pointed out.

"But I had my lunch not half an hour ago," the

Professor said, "at six o'clock precisely, which would suggest, although not prove conclusively, that it is neither the morning nor the evening, but the early afternoon. On the other hand, if you could supply me with some empirical evidence that refutes my contention, then I would be forced to amend my thesis."

"Er. . ." said Arthur.

"Professor, may I introduce you to Arthur Holmwood?" Jack asked. "Arthur is Lucy's fiancé."

"Pleased to meet you," Arthur said, shaking the Professor by the hand. "I'm very grateful to you for coming such a long way to see Lucy."

"Well," said the Professor, "I have to be honest and say that I was utterly absorbed in my fascinating research into the saprophytic agaricaceous poisonous woodland fungus, *Amanita muscaria*. I nearly couldn't tear myself away."

"Er, quite," said Arthur. "I don't blame you," he added after a slight pause.

"I was at a crucial stage, too," mused the Professor regretfully. "Normally nothing could have induced me to abandon everything at a moment's notice. But when I got Jack's telegram I felt I had little choice. The symptoms he described are very worrying indeed. I suppose the situation is still the same, Jack?"

"I'm afraid it's much worse," Jack responded.

When the Professor saw Lucy, he clenched his jaw. She was as pale as chalk, and the bones of her face were standing out prominently.

"Professor Van Helsing, please *do* something!" Arthur begged.

The Professor began to make his examination.

"Jack," he said after a while, "do you know how she came to lose so much blood?"

"But she hasn't lost any blood."

"Oh, she has. Believe me, she has. And unless it is replaced, she may die. It's lucky she has a common blood group. There must be an immediate transfusion." He turned to Arthur, who had sat down heavily in a chair and put his head in his hands. "Are you willing to help the young lady?"

"I would give the last drop of blood in my body for her."

"You may have to," the Professor said grimly.

Professor Van Helsing asked Arthur to sit by the bed and roll his sleeve up. He took a sample of blood, checking it was from the same blood group as Lucy's. Then he performed the transfusion swiftly and efficiently. As the blood flowed from Arthur to Lucy, a touch of pink began to return to her cheeks. The Professor carefully monitored the situation.

"Enough. Jack, attend to the young man while I see to the lady. He needs to lie down somewhere. But he can be assured that he has saved his fiancée's life today."

Arthur was feeling rather groggy, so Jack helped him to his feet. But just as he was supporting him to the bedroom door, there was a sudden hiss of shock from the Professor.

"What is it?" Jack called.

"Look after your friend, then come back as quickly as you can," was the reply.

As soon as Jack was sure that Arthur was all right, he rushed back upstairs.

"Does Lucy always wear this black velvet band around her neck?" the Professor asked.

"I don't know," Jack said. "I can't remember – why?"

The Professor pushed the band down. On the side of Lucy's throat were two small wounds.

"What do you make of that?" he asked.

Jack examined the red marks.

"I'm not sure. I've never seen anything like it. There's no sign of disease or infection. And yet. . ."

"And yet what?"

"The wounds don't look clean. They look as though they keep being reopened."

"They are being reopened. Every night. That's how she is losing all her blood."

Jack racked his brains for an illness or disease which would explain it. He couldn't think of one.

"But how is it happening?" he asked.

"There isn't time to tell you now," the Professor said, busily putting all his medical equipment away. "As soon as I got your telegram I had my small suspicions. The unusually pale skin, the difficulty in breathing, the dreams of bats, of wolves. . . They all pointed to the same conclusion."

"But what conclusion?" Jack asked.

"Now that I have seen her," the Professor said, ignoring him, "my small suspicions have become very great fears indeed."

"But fears of what?"

"And now, Jack, I must read. I have brought all the books I could find on this. . . this subject. Now I must read all about it."

"But what subject is it?"

"And I must find more books, from the libraries, from the British Museum. I must read all night. And you, Jack, have to stay here and watch over Lucy. You mustn't leave her, not even for a moment. Do you understand?"

"Well of course I understand," Jack replied rather crossly, "but surely you can just tell me –"

But the Professor was already out of the door.

That evening, after Lucy's mother had sat with them for a while, Jack took care of his patient. Lucy seemed afraid of going to sleep, so he promised to stay awake all night, and to wake her if she seemed to be having a nightmare. She soon fell into a deep sleep. Jack watched over her tenderly. Sometimes, as the big, old grandfather clock downstairs chimed away the hours of the night, he couldn't help feeling sad, thinking about what might have been. Ever since Lucy had turned down his marriage proposal, Jack's life had been work, work, and more work as he threw himself into the running of the hospital.

But he tried hard not to let himself become too miserable. After all, the only thing that really mattered was Lucy's health.

The next evening Professor Van Helsing returned to Hillingham. He was covered from head to foot in dust, and was carrying a large parcel.

"The books I've read in your excellent libraries!" he exclaimed. "Some of them hadn't been opened for two hundred years! I've been reading non-stop, all night and all day. How is our patient?"

"Come and see for yourself," Jack replied.

"Good evening, Professor," Lucy said brightly when they went to her room. "I've heard all about you from Arthur. I want to thank you for your treatment."

"Ah, good," said the Professor contentedly. She was still a little pale and weak, but she looked much better. "It was your young man who saved your life, my dear."

"Arthur," Lucy said.

"Yes, Arthur. It was all down to him. Where is he today?"

"His father is ill and has taken a turn for the worse," Lucy replied. "Arthur has gone to look after him."

"So much misfortune," the Professor murmured. "But here, at least, I hope there will be no more. I think I know the cause of your illness. And once the cause is known, the treatment can be found."

"What's wrong with her?" Jack asked quietly.

The Professor smiled sadly, but said nothing. Instead, he unwrapped his parcel and produced a large bundle of white flowers.

"These are for you, Miss Lucy."

"For me? Oh!" Lucy sniffed them, but then drew her head back, wrinkling her nose in disgust. "Yuk! They smell like garlic!"

"They are garlic flowers," said the Professor. "They will keep you safe from −" but then he stopped himself.

"From what?" Lucy asked.

"From the evil of your illness, my dear."

Before the Professor and Jack left that night for some much needed rest, they arranged the garlic flowers in Lucy's room. Under the Professor's direction, Jack made sure that all the windows were firmly shut, before rubbing the flowers around the door and windows. The Professor made up a garland from the flowers, and carefully put it around Lucy's neck.

"This will be your medicine," he told her. "There will be no more bad dreams, as long as you wear this. And remember − don't open the windows on any account, not even if it gets hot and stuffy."

"I won't," Lucy told him as she settled down to sleep. "Thank you so much for your help. I somehow feel much safer now. I can't wait until I'm better."

"You'll be out and about with Arthur in no time," said the Professor.

The Professor was in excellent spirits when he and Jack returned to Hillingham early the following day.

"Good morning to you, Mrs. Westenra!" he boomed when Lucy's mother opened the door.

"And good morning to you, Professor."

"And how is your beautiful daughter today? Much better no doubt after my first-class treatment!"

Mrs. Westenra smiled proudly.

"Well, Professor, if Lucy is better this morning, it will be down to my care as well as your treatment."

"Oh yes?" said the Professor, rubbing his hands together cheerfully.

"You see, I went into Lucy's room in the middle of the night, and there she was, fast asleep, as peaceful as a baby."

"Good, good," the Professor said, and he clapped Jack over the shoulder. "I knew my diagnosis was right!"

"But I happen to know a thing or two about nursing. In my day I was renowned for my abilities in nursing. In fact, it would be no exaggeration to say that I know more about nursing than —"

"I'm sure your nursing abilities are beyond comparison," Jack said kindly.

"Beyond comparison," Mrs. Westenra agreed. "I couldn't put it better myself, Jack. Quite simply, they are beyond comparison. And as it was terribly stuffy in Lucy's room, I decided to —"

The Professor's face went ashen.

"— to open the window," Mrs. Westenra said.

"Really Professor, I'm surprised at you. Fresh air is essential to a convalescing patient."

"It might not matter," muttered the Professor. "Just as long as the garland wasn't removed. . ."

"And as for all those horrible-smelling flowers," Mrs. Westenra continued, "you'll be glad to know that I took them and threw them out. You see, when your nursing abilities are beyond comparison, as mine are, then you understand how —"

But Jack and the Professor weren't listening. They were rushing up the stairs to Lucy's room. They found Lucy unconscious, more horribly white and wan than before. The skin on her face seemed to have shrunk, so that she had a gaunt, skeletal look, and she hardly seemed able to breathe.

"My God!" Jack whispered, sinking to his knees by her side. "What happened in the night?"

The Professor turned his medicine bag upside down and tipped the contents onto the floor.

"Roll your sleeve up!" he shouted. "She needs more blood! Mine's the wrong blood group but yours will do!"

For the second time in twenty-four hours, he performed a blood transfusion. As Jack watched his own blood being pumped into Lucy's veins, he wondered how on earth she had lost so much so quickly. Not from those two small wounds on her neck, surely? If so, where had it all gone?

The two men stayed with Lucy all day. The second transfusion didn't strengthen her as much as the first, and she was still quite weak by the evening. Jack felt weak too, but he sat with her while Professor Van Helsing went to talk to Mrs. Westenra. He wanted to make absolutely sure that she wouldn't disturb the garlic flowers that night. On his return, he and Jack arranged the flowers as before. Jack made doubly sure that all the windows were securely shut, and the Professor made an extra-large garland for Lucy's neck.

"I think we should watch over her, too," Jack suggested. "I'd feel better if we did."

"Jack, the garlic will protect her. You have given so much blood today, you need to rest. And I, I need to seek out more books. I must read. There is so much I must find out about this, this monstrosity. There are things you don't understand, Jack. If I told you, you just wouldn't believe me. Our only friend is knowledge. Now, let me put you in a carriage and send you home."

Lucy couldn't sleep that night. From the garden outside there was a howl, like a dog's, but fiercer and harsher. Shakily, she got out of bed and went over to the window. She couldn't see much outside – just a big bat flitting about. As she watched, it came up to the window, buffeting its wings against the glass. Lucy didn't like it. She got back into bed and decided to stay awake. She kept feeling at the garland of garlic around her neck, to reassure herself that it was still there.

Eventually she must have drifted off, because some hours later she woke up. She gave a little cry of fright. She couldn't see anything, but she could sense that someone was in the room. She peered into the darkness with dread, her heart thumping, and her forehead damp with sweat.

"Who's there?" she said. There was a short silence, and then a noise, a sort of scary, rustling noise, just inches away from her bed. Lucy's whole body began to tremble.

"Who's there?" she called again.

"I'm afraid I can't sleep," Mrs. Westenra said.

"Mother!" Lucy exclaimed in relief, sinking back on her pillows.

"There's such a terrible wind blowing outside," Mrs. Westenra said. "It's really frightening me."

She snuggled up beside Lucy, and the two of them listened to the sound of the wind.

"What's that other noise?" Mrs. Westenra whispered.

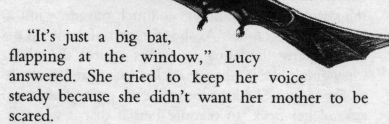

"It's just a big bat, flapping at the window," Lucy answered. She tried to keep her voice steady because she didn't want her mother to be scared.

"I don't like bats!" Mrs. Westenra cried. "I hate bats! Is it a very big bat? I bet it's a huge bat! It's probably as big as an eagle!"

"Hush," Lucy soothed her, "try not to be frightened."

But even as she spoke, a strange sort of moaning sound came from the garden. It started quietly, almost softly, but then grew louder and more mournful, until it became an ear-shattering, appalling howl. It went on and on and on, and Mrs. Westenra whimpered with terror and pulled the sheets up to her nose. Suddenly the wind dropped, and the howling stopped with it. The moon must have come out from under a cloud, because the whole room flooded with light. There was a split second of absolute quiet. Then with a tremendous crash the bedroom window shattered, and there, in the window frame, looking through the jagged panes, was the enormous head of a great, red-eyed wolf.

Kenston

Mrs. Westenra shrieked and wailed. Her hands began grabbing at everything around her – the sheets, the bedside table, Lucy – and in her terror she clutched at Lucy's throat, pulling off the garland of garlic. For a second or two she sat up, pointing at the wolf, and a strange gurgling noise came from her throat. Then she fainted, falling out of the bed and striking her head on the bedside table as she slumped to the floor.

Almost against her will, Lucy's eyes were fixed on the wolf. For a moment both she and the huge, vicious beast were absolutely still. Then the creature's head drew back a little. It seemed to break up into millions of little specks which all charged about in a mass. The specks came blowing in through the broken window, beginning to take on the shape of a sinister figure.

Desperately Lucy scrabbled for something to defend herself with, her hands groping uselessly over the books and pens on her bedside table, scattering them all over. She clutched the edges of the bed and stared in terror. Then she screamed.

Desperate Measures

Jack woke that morning to the sound of wheels clattering over cobblestones. He went to the window and leaned out. Four large carts, each drawn by four horses, were lumbering past the hospital. As he watched, he heard one of the patients shrieking a strange chant through the bars of his window:

> *"Tyrant of the human race,*
> *Master of all evil powers,*
> *Welcome to this gloomy place,*
> *Lie here safe in daylight hours."*

Each cart was loaded with large wooden boxes. Jack wondered why they were heading for Carfax, the deserted old ruin next door.

> *"Lord of horror, king of fear,*
> *Sleeping on your mound of mud,*
> *Spread your terror far and near,*
> *Seek your prey and suck their blood!"*

It sounded like Renfield, the most dangerous and unpredictable inmate in the hospital. His gruesome rhymes were fascinating to Jack, but there was no time to investigate. The Professor's advice about rest had been all very well, but now he wanted to get back to Hillingham as quickly as possible.

No one answered when he knocked on the big old door half an hour later. He tried again, and waited for a long time. Still no answer. While he was standing there, bemused, a carriage drew up and the Professor jumped out eagerly.

"Good morning, Jack! I've read over 400,000 words in just under twelve hours! About 395,000 of them were completely useless, but I did learn something very interesting about –"

"No one is answering the door," Jack interrupted. "There's probably a good reason, but I don't like it."

The two men walked around the building. The doors and windows were all firmly shut. Before long they found themselves back at the front door again.

"Now what?" Jack asked.

As he spoke, he saw Mrs. Westenra's maid and cook hurrying up the street.

"We can't get in!" the cook cried. "We've come back every half hour since six, but there's still no answer!"

The Professor took a long, thin knife from his medicine bag and started to attack one of the windows.

"Why didn't I listen to you, Jack?" he cried, as he worked the blade under the wood. After a while he managed to lever the window open. Jack scrambled through it and ran upstairs.

Lucy's bedroom door was closed. He pushed it open a few inches, wondering what he would find inside. He could hear the Professor coming up behind him, panting. Jack gave the heavy oak door a firm push. It swung open on its hinges, striking the wall with a dull thud. Standing side by side, Jack and the Professor looked at the scene of desolation inside.

"No. . ." Jack breathed.

Mrs. Westenra was dead. She was lying on the floor inside a circle of broken glass, her eyes wide open and an expression of terror fixed on her face. And as for Lucy. . . Jack closed his eyes tightly, as if to make the horror go away. She lay motionless on the bed, spotted with blood. Her face was as white as snow. There were more drops of blood on the floor between the bed and the broken window, where the curtains were flapping in the breeze.

For one more moment Jack and the Professor stood, transfixed by the gruesome spectacle. Then they came to their senses and ran to Lucy's side.

"Is she dead?" Jack cried.

The Professor pulled back her eyelids to look into her eyes, then felt for her pulse. At first he couldn't feel anything. And then –

"She's alive – just! Get me some brandy – quick!"

"Thank God!" Jack whispered, and he scrabbled around in his medicine bag for brandy.

"She feels like ice," the Professor said, pouring brandy between Lucy's lips. "We need hot water, and a hot fire. We must warm her up!"

"Do you think she's going to die?" Jack whispered.

The Professor looked up at him grimly as he rubbed Lucy's arms.

"God help us if she does."

"Why do you say that?"

"Have you seen her teeth?" the Professor asked.

Jack gasped. The tips of two sharp teeth were just visible at the corners of Lucy's mouth.

"Her teeth are – growing!" He recoiled in disgust. "Professor, what *is* this illness?"

The Professor didn't answer, but handed Jack a piece of paper.

"This was in her hand," he said. "She is a brave young woman. She was writing it out even as. . . even as. . ." He paused. "She wanted us to know what happened."

Jack flattened out the crumpled piece of paper. In a large, untidy scrawl, written as though in a desperate hurry, were the letters:

VAM

"What does it mean?"

But the Professor just shook his head, and started rubbing Lucy's limbs even harder.

Professor Van Helsing and Jack struggled hard to save Lucy. After her maid had given her a hot bath, she was placed in front of the fireplace in her bedroom, where they had built up a roaring fire. But she remained freezing cold. Unless she became warmer, another blood transfusion was simply out of the question. And without another transfusion, she wouldn't live long.

"Send for her young man," said the Professor said, putting his arm around Jack's shoulder. Jack covered his face with his hands. "She's leaving us soon."

When Arthur arrived and saw Lucy, he couldn't speak. He sat at her bedside, holding her hand and talking to her in a low voice. Jack and the Professor left them alone.

"In the middle of so much sadness," the Professor said softly to his grieving friend, "it's good to keep busy. And there's so much to do. For instance, imagine how grateful Miss Lucy would be if she knew that someone was dealing with all the funeral arrangements for her mother. Someone she cared about and trusted."

Jack smiled sadly.

"You're quite right," he said. "Arthur's in no fit state at the moment. And have you seen all that unopened mail in the hall? Someone should go through it."

"Good idea."

Jack kept himself occupied as the Professor had suggested. After dealing with a few invoices and receipts, he opened a hand-written letter from Mina. Jack knew Mina quite well. The last he had heard, she had gone abroad to look after her sick fiancé.

Dearest Lucy,

Here we are, back in England! Jonathan is my husband, and I'm his wife. We were married in Budapest. Jonathan is stronger and beginning to put some flesh on his bones. It's true that he wakes up sometimes in the middle of the night, screaming about. . . Well, perhaps I shouldn't say. The important thing is, every day he's a little bit better.

And what about you? When is the wedding to be? I expect it will be more of an occasion than mine, which took place in a hospital bedroom! Jonathan and I think of you and Arthur often. We wish you a long and happy life together, and hope that you will be as happy as we are. Looking forward to hearing from you soon.

Much love,
Mina xxx

Jack blinked back tears as he began writing a letter to Mina informing her of the terrible events at Hillingham. *I am afraid I have to inform you that Mrs. Westenra is dead,* he wrote, *and our dear friend Lucy is dying. . .*

In the study, the Professor settled down in an armchair and opened an ancient volume: *The Manifestations of the Vampire.* He was just reading the first paragraph when Arthur burst into the room.

"Professor, come quickly!"

"What is it?" asked the Professor.

"She's talking and moving around. She looks much stronger. There's still hope!" Arthur declared.

The Professor followed Arthur to Lucy's room. Lucy was sitting up in bed. Her lips were pulled back into a ghastly smile. The two sharp teeth seemed even longer than before. She was breathing in heavy gasps, sometimes breaking into mirthless laughter.

"See!" Arthur said.

Jack, who had heard all the commotion and followed them, stared in astonishment. It hardly seemed possible that someone as sick as Lucy could sit up in bed, laughing. But on the other hand, she hardly looked like Lucy any more. It was as though somebody else was pretending to be Lucy.

"The wounds on her neck – " the Professor hissed. "They've gone! This is one of the signs I've read about!"

Suddenly, Lucy shook her head, so that her long hair came loose, cascading over her shoulders. She laughed again, scornfully. Earlier in the day the Professor had placed a cross on a chain around her neck. Now she grabbed the chain and broke it, flinging the cross to the floor. Then they heard her say, in a soft, deep voice utterly unlike her own, "Arthur, my love! Kiss me!"

Arthur, desperate to believe that Lucy was going to recover, bent over her eagerly to kiss her. But in an instant Professor Van Helsing, old man that he was, caught hold of him and hurled him across the room.

"No! For the sake of your life and your soul, no!"

Sat on the floor where the Professor had thrown him, Arthur looked up, bewildered and angry.

"Professor," Jack asked, "what are you doing? What's going on?"

The Professor didn't answer, watching closely as Lucy sank down on the bed. Her eyes closed, and her breathing became quieter. Then she opened her eyes once more. This time she looked like the real Lucy, and although she was terribly weak, she held out her hand to the Professor, who grasped it in his own.

"My true, true friend," she whispered, "and Arthur's." Her voice was weak, but it was her own voice. Summoning what was left of her strength, she made one last, supreme effort to speak.

"Professor. . . you must defeat. . . this. . . evil."

"I will, I swear!" the Professor whispered.

Then he turned to Arthur.

"Now you can hold her hand, and say goodbye."

Arthur came to Lucy's side. He gently took her hand in his own, and they gazed into each other's eyes. After a few minutes, Lucy's eyes closed, her breathing ceased, and time itself seemed to stand still.

"She's gone, Arthur," Jack said eventually, placing his hand on his silent friend's shoulder. "She's at peace now. This is the end."

But the Professor, wiping his eyes, shook his head.

"No, this is not the end," he muttered to himself. "This is only the beginning. . ."

The funeral of Lucy and Mrs. Westenra took place several days later, and was the most miserable morning any of Lucy's friends had ever experienced. Both Arthur and Jack were very brave, and did not break down. They spent a lot of time talking to Mina, who had come down to London with Jonathan, and in their own ways they all gave each other some comfort. But there was no mistaking the despair they felt. It seemed to hang in the air itself.

After the service, Mina and Jonathan had some spare time before going home. They went for a long, slow, sad walk through Hyde Park. They had stopped for a few minutes to rest when Jonathan grabbed Mina's arm so tightly that it hurt.

"No!" he breathed.

"What is it?" Mina cried out in alarm.

"It's him," Jonathan groaned, "and he looks younger than ever!"

"Who?"

"That vile monster, from Transylvania. . ." Jonathan couldn't go on. He seemed half amazed and half terrified, and his face took on a ghostly pallor. Mina followed the line of his gaze. She found that she was looking at a tall, thin man, dressed

entirely in black, with a very pale face and jet-black hair. He was staring at a young woman who was walking along the path. His cruel mouth formed a sneer as she passed him, and Mina saw two big white teeth, as long as a wolf's and sharper than needles. As the dark figure turned to follow the woman, a red light flashed from his eyes. Watching his retreating back, a vivid memory came back to Mina. It was a memory of Lucy, sleeping on the bench on the East Cliff in Whitby, while a strange figure loomed over her. A figure with flashing red eyes. . . Was it possible that, somehow, there was a link between Lucy's illness and whatever had happened to Jonathan in Transylvania?

Mina made a quick decision. She was going to read Jonathan's journal. Only then would she be able to understand what he had gone through. Perhaps it would help to explain Lucy's death as well. Then she thought about the odd little scientist she had met at the funeral, Professor Van Helsing, who kept muttering to himself about defeating the forces of evil. There was something compelling about him. Perhaps it would be a good idea to show him the journal too. Maybe he would be able to help her unravel the mystery.

After Lucy's funeral, Professor Van Helsing showed no inclination to return to Amsterdam. Instead, he stayed at the hospital with Jack. While Jack attended to his patients, the Professor studied his books; old, dusty books, crumbling to pieces, such as *Vampire Arts, The Unknown Powers,* and *Conquering The Undead.*

One evening, as the two men were relaxing in the study after a hard day's work, the Professor began reading the newspaper.

"Ah!" he suddenly exclaimed.

"What is it?" Jack asked.

"So soon, so soon," his friend murmured sadly as he read. Then he looked at Jack. "Do you know why I chose to stay here, rather than return to Amsterdam?"

"No," said Jack. "I would have thought you had a lot of work to do in Amsterdam."

"I do. But the reason I stay here is contained in this article. Listen to this: *'Panic is growing in the Hampstead area because of a series of unusual attacks. Several victims have been discovered on Hampstead Heath in the past few days, half-conscious, deathly pale, and each with a distinctive injury — two small wounds on the throat. Although the victims appear to recover after a day or two, doctors are mystified as to the nature of their illness.'* Well, Jack. What do you think about that?"

"I don't know what to make of it," Jack said. "The injuries are like Lucy's, but as to the cause. . ."

The Professor paused before speaking.

"I know exactly what, or rather, I know exactly *who* has caused these injuries on Hampstead Heath."

Jack sat bolt upright in his chair.

"Who? Perhaps Lucy's injuries were made by the same person!" he said excitedly.

"That's impossible," the Professor answered.

"Why?"

"Try not to be angry with me, Jack, when I tell you this. The time has come when you must believe the unbelievable. The person who made these recent attacks. . . was Lucy."

Jack stood up, knocking his chair over.

"Are you out of your mind?" he raged. "Lucy is *dead!*"

"If only I were out of my mind," the Professor sighed. "I would happily be mad, like one of your poor patients, if that could change the agony of the truth."

"And what evidence do you have," Jack said sarcastically, "for this, this obscene accusation?"

"Come with me to her tomb tonight, and I will show you the evidence."

Jack glared at him in even more anger and disbelief.

"Never! I'd rather die than show such disrespect to the woman I. . . to a person who. . . to Lucy!"

The Professor nodded.

"I do not blame you for being angry. But at least read this," he said, passing him a notebook. "It's Jonathan Harker's journal of his stay in Transylvania. Mina Harker sent it to me after her husband broke down in Hyde Park. I assure you, as I assured her, that every word of it is true. Read it, and then come back. If you still refuse to come tonight, then I'll never mention this painful issue again. If I have to," he muttered grimly, "I'll fight the monster alone."

Without a word, Jack snatched the notebook from him and stamped out of the room. The Professor sank back in his chair heavily and closed his eyes. At that moment, in the middle of so much pain and distress, all he wanted to do was sleep. But before ten minutes had passed, Jack had come back into the room.

"Professor, get ready. We're all going to the graveyard."

The Graveyard

The graveyard was only a short distance from Hampstead Heath, and as the last lingering light of the day was fading, Jack and the Professor went there by carriage. Checking that no one was around, they scaled the sturdy iron railings. The graveyard was overgrown and neglected. Vast yew trees and cedars had spread their roots under the packed headstones and forgotten memorials, toppling many of them to the ground. Thousands of people were buried there, and as the two men made their way to the vault of the Westenra family, it felt like every one of them was watching.

"How are we going to get in?" Jack asked as they stood by the black metal door to the vault.

"I'm afraid that I bribed the undertaker's assistant," the Professor admitted, inserting a large, rusty key into the lock.

Jack began to have second thoughts. Could they really be sure that they were doing the right thing? What if it wasn't Lucy who was stalking the Heath? In that case, they were committing a very serious crime. He watched unhappily as the door slowly opened. In the stillness of the graveyard, the creaking of the hinges sounded as loud as a scream.

"I don't like it," he said. "We're disturbing the dead."

The Professor smiled grimly. He struck a match, lit a candle, then turned to face the interior of the vault.

"Remember Jonathan's journal, Jack. Whatever else we're doing," he said gravely over his shoulder, "I can assure you that we're not disturbing the dead."

They climbed down thirteen stone steps and entered the vault. It was easy to see which coffin was Lucy's, because it was surrounded by flowers. Sadly, Jack watched the candlelight flicker over the wreath he had provided. In the middle of the dying blooms he could still make out the words he had written:

To Lucy, a friend I will never forget.

The Professor began to loosen the coffin lid with a screwdriver.

"What are you doing?" Jack whispered. "If opening Lucy's coffin isn't disturbing her peace, what is?"

The Professor didn't answer, continuing to unscrew the lid as quickly as he could, as if he were afraid that Jack might try to stop him. Jack stepped back. He knew that a week-old corpse would be an unpleasant sight. He waited to hear the hiss of gas seeping from the coffin, the gas produced by decomposing flesh. The Professor seemed entirely unconcerned about this danger. He lifted the heavy lid slowly but surely, without even looking inside.

Then he held the candle over the coffin.

"Take a look, Jack. Tell me what you see."

Jack took a deep breath.

"I. . . I can't."

"You must!" the Professor urged him.

"I can't – you know why! I can't bear to see her!"

"Perhaps you won't have to," said the Professor, enigmatically. "You must look, Jack."

Jack felt a terrible dread consume him as as he stepped forward. What would Lucy look like, ravaged by her illness, consumed by death? Little by little he edged slightly nearer and finally, with infinite reluctance, he looked inside. For some moments he stood motionless, just staring. Then his face contorted into an expression of pure bewilderment. He turned to the Professor, shaking his head, then looked again.

The coffin was empty.

"This is proof," the Professor announced, "if you needed any more proof, that Lucy is now. . ."

"Is now what, Professor?" Jack whispered.

"One of the Undead, such as Jonathan Harker described in his journal."

The words tore into Jack's heart and mind like raw, physical pain, making him clutch the sides of the coffin to stop himself from falling to his knees. Lucy, the woman he had loved, was a vampire!

"She isn't the real Lucy," the Professor continued, "just a tragic, evil thing, which must be destroyed. We'll return tomorrow night with Arthur. We have to convince him of what we know before we carry out this dreadful duty."

"Arthur!" Jack exclaimed, the absurdity of the idea giving him his voice back. "You can't expect Arthur to come here! Think about it, Professor. She was his fiancée!"

Professor Van Helsing stood up straight, gripped Jack's arm, and spoke so quietly, yet so firmly, that Jack felt like he was back at medical school again, in one of the Professor's lectures.

"For the sake of Lucy's soul, and for all humanity, this thing must be destroyed. But we can't expect Arthur to understand if he hasn't seen it for himself. He must come. And I know how to make him."

"NO!" Arthur bellowed the next morning, striking the table with his fist. "No, no and no again!"

"I'm sorry, Arthur," said the Professor sadly, "to involve you in such a painful request. I know that it must be hard for you to understand. I can only tell you that, if you come with us this evening, you'll know why I'm asking."

"What do you want to do there?" Arthur asked.

"Drive a sharpened stake through her heart," said the Professor, almost casually.

Arthur's eyes nearly popped out of his head.

"I forbid it," he hissed. "If you even speak of it again, you'll have me to answer to." With that he left the room, slamming the door behind him.

The following night, as a full moon hung over Hampstead Heath, the Professor and Jack could be found hiding behind some tombstones in the graveyard. They were keeping watch over the Westenra family vault. A little farther away a third man was hiding. It was Arthur. The Professor's suggestion had appalled him so much that he had followed them. If they went anywhere near the door of the tomb, they'd have him to deal with.

Shuffling from one foot to the other, Arthur accidentally stood on a stick. It made a loud crack! Jack's heart raced and pounded when he heard it, and he peered into the night, anxiously waiting for the horrible approach of. . . he smiled to himself rather sheepishly, suddenly realizing that he didn't know what might be making a horrible approach. The Professor heard the noise too, and smiled for a different reason. It was good to know that his plan had worked, and that he had provoked Arthur into following them.

The three men waited for ages. The night seemed to get colder and darker, and Jack began to get more and more impatient. What was the Professor thinking of, making him stand in a graveyard half the night when he could be curled up under a warm eiderdown? And anyway, what were they here for? They already knew that Lucy's body had gone. It wasn't as if it was going to come marching across the graveyard, open the door of the vault, get back inside the coffin and settle down for a quick nap. Was it?

"Pssssst!"

Jack looked up, startled, to see that the Professor was pointing at something. Some distance away, flitting between the headstones, was a dim white shape. As he watched, the wind dropped, creating an eerie silence. It was difficult to see what the white thing was, but it was getting nearer and nearer, slowly but surely, and as it did so Jack saw that it was holding something. He strained his eyes, trying to make out what it was. The pale, mysterious figure climbed onto a raised tomb. At that moment, a moment which would be engraved forever in the memories of the three watching men, the moon came out, illuminating a horrible sight with a cold, blue light.

On the raised tomb, her white dress smeared with fresh blood, stood Lucy. The eyes which had once been clear and friendly were like sizzling flames. Her lips curled and slobbered like the jowls of a starving dog. Blood trickled from her vampire teeth onto her chin, before dripping onto the bundle she carried in her arms – it was a boy, a teenage boy. She bent her head down over his throat, saliva dripping from her lips. Her mouth opened, and for an instant her teeth glinted like daggers. She seemed to wait for a few seconds, relishing the prospect of sinking her teeth into his neck. And it was then that the Professor made his move. He stepped out from behind the yew tree to stand in front of her silently. Following his lead, Jack emerged from his hiding place, and Arthur stumbled out of the undergrowth to join them. They stood in a triangle in front of the Westenra family vault, the Professor in front and the other two behind.

When Lucy – or the thing that now bore Lucy's shape – saw them, she snarled like an animal. Her eyes ranged over them; first the Professor, then Jack, and then. . . as she looked at Arthur, her mouth formed into a cruel smile. She laughed, deep and loud, and with a sudden careless gesture dropped the boy to the ground. Seeing his chance, the boy scampered away and hid behind a tree. The Professor breathed a sigh of relief. The legions of the Undead had just lost their newest recruit.

Lucy sprang down from the tomb. Advancing upon them, she seemed simultaneously horrible and lovely, appealing and appalling. Arthur's eyes widened as she came closer. She stopped in front of them, wiped some blood from the corner of her mouth with her arm, and smiled again.

"Arthur. . ." she breathed in a soft, sweet, seductive voice, "Arthur, come to me. . ."

She stretched out her arms to him, and Arthur put his head in his hands and sobbed.

"Arthur. . ." she breathed again, her voice even softer, even sweeter.

Trembling, Arthur looked at her through his fingers, and instead of a vicious monster, stained with blood, he saw Lucy. His hands slipped slowly down his face. Then he reached out to her.

"Lucy!"

It was just as she smirked in triumph that the Professor stepped between them, holding out a small, gold crucifix.

Jack blinked in astonishment at the speed of the vampire's reaction. She recoiled as if struck by a bolt of lightning, her expression becoming one of baffled malice. She hissed like a snake, but she was utterly powerless. The Professor watched, unflinching.

"Arthur," he said finally, "do you understand now? Do I have your permission to go on with my work?"

"Do as you want, Professor," Arthur moaned, throwing himself onto his knees. "I understand nothing except horror and misery!"

"Things will get better," said the Professor gently, "when we have done what we have to do."

Cautiously he moved nearer to Lucy. Her eyes blazed with fury, but the powers of the crucifix were greater than her vampire powers, and she backed away.

"Get Arthur away from the vault," the Professor told Jack. "You're about to see something rather interesting."

Holding the crucifix in front of him, he slowly circled Lucy until there was nothing between her and the vault. With a grisly grin, she backed away to the black metal door. Then her body seemed to fade into tiny specks, forming a floating shape which slipped under the narrow crack at the bottom of the door. The vampire had returned to the dark sanctuary of her grave.

Stepping up to the door while Jack and Arthur still stood blinking in astonishment, the Professor began to seal it with a sort of paste.

"My own invention," he said proudly. "Putty mixed with garlic." He patted the substance into the cracks until there wasn't even the smallest gap left.

"Now she can't escape," he said, "and in the daytime, when she's sleeping, we'll return. But first we must look after that poor young boy. Jack, will you take him home? There are things I must explain to Arthur."

When they returned to the graveyard in the daylight there were several funerals taking place. They watched as a family mourned at an open grave. They waited until the last funeral was over before making their way cautiously to the vault. Jack squeezed Arthur's arm as they followed the Professor down into its darkness. At the very bottom, the Professor lit a candle.

"Remember what I told you, Arthur, and do not flinch from your task."

Arthur gasped when the lid was open. There was Lucy. In the quiet of her grave, resting from the horrible impulses which made her stalk the night for blood, she was beautiful. Her eyes were closed, her expression serene.

"Is she really dead?" Arthur breathed.

"No, she is not dead. That's the point," the Professor said sternly. "Would someone who had been dead for more than a week look as lovely as this? She is one of the Undead, and her soul will never rest until we release it from this evil curse."

The Professor took a thick wooden stake out of a bag. It was as long as his arm, with one end sharpened to a point. He laid it on the floor, and next to it placed a heavy hammer. Then he stepped back, waiting for Arthur to pick the implements up. Momentarily, Arthur hesitated.

"The Undead do not die," the Professor said quietly. "They go on, age after age, attacking new victims and multiplying the evils of the world. Their souls are in torment. Arthur, Lucy needs you to perform an act of great love and great courage. For although the Undead do not die, they can be killed."

Arthur stepped forward.

"I'm ready," he said.

He picked up the heavy stake with one hand and the hammer with the other.

"Place the point of the stake over her heart," the Professor said, "raise the hammer high, and summon all your strength. Then do what has to be done."

The Professor took a small book from his pocket and began to recite a prayer. The ancient words of worship echoed around the stone chamber as Arthur held the hammer high in the air. Jack watched the light of the candle flame shine on its dull metal. He crossed himself and bowed his head. Then Arthur struck the stake as hard as he could.

The thing in the coffin quivered, writhing and thrashing from side to side. A hideous, bloodcurdling screech came from its open lips. It shook and twisted wildly, its face contorted in agony.

"Again!" shouted the Professor over the gruesome noise, "again!"

Arthur delivered a second tremendous blow. There was a last, horrible squeal. The writhing of the body stopped. The vampire was dead.

While he was performing this terrible task, Arthur hadn't faltered. Now it was done, the hammer fell from his grip, and he fell backward. Jack caught him, and lowered him to the floor. The strain had been too much. For a few minutes, Jack and the Professor were so busy looking after him that they didn't look in the coffin. But when they did, they stared in wonder.

"So we did the right thing," Jack said.

"Did you doubt it?" asked the Professor.

Together they gently pulled Arthur to his feet and helped him to the coffin. The foul thing that had taken over Lucy's body had gone, and in its place lay the real Lucy. Her face was ravaged with illness and the marks of pain and suffering, but her expression was as human and gentle as they remembered.

"Now Lucy really is dead," said the Professor solemnly. "Her soul is at peace and in heaven, where you will surely meet her again, Arthur."

Two days later, in his study at the hospital, Jack was sitting at the table frowning in concentration. Next to him was Mina. Opposite them sat Arthur and Jonathan. And at the head of the table, standing up, the Professor was addressing them. He had called them all together for an important meeting.

"One part of our work is over," he was saying. "But a greater task remains. It is to seek out the author of all our sorrow. And then. . ." He paused, looking slowly at the expectant faces in front of him.

"And then kill him," Jonathan said vehemently, to murmurs of agreement. Now that the battle was finally out in the open, Jonathan had regained all his old strength and spirit. He no longer felt like the only person in the world who knew about Dracula. He was part of a team.

"We all know what happened to poor Lucy," the Professor gravely said, "and those of you who weren't already familiar with Jonathan's journal have now read it. Very few people," he said with admiration, "have faced what he has faced and lived to tell the tale. His journal provides an invaluable insight into the powers and habits of this scourge on humanity."

He began to pace up and down the length of the study, stroking his chin thoughtfully.

"I have made it my task to learn as much as possible about the many dangers we face. Jack will testify to the days and nights I have spent in this room, in that chair, reading books and papers untouched for centuries. My purpose in calling this meeting is to share my knowledge – my knowledge of Dracula."

Abruptly he stopped pacing up and down, stood behind his chair and thumped the table.

"There are such beings as vampires. Dracula is the greatest and most evil vampire there has ever been. He is as strong as twenty men and has the cunning that comes from living over a thousand years. He is able to change his form to any beast. He can –"

"So that huge dog which leapt from the ship in Whitby was Dracula!" Mina suddenly interrupted.

"Correct. And he has other tricks. He can control the weather, causing fogs and winds and storms. He can control all animals which live in groups – rats, bats, wolves, wild dogs. He casts no shadow, and has no reflection in water or mirrors. He can fade into a million specks and disappear. These are his powers. As to his purpose, all of us here know what that is. It is to suck blood, the blood of the young, and so add to the numbers of the Undead and perpetuate his own youth."

"I want this monster dead as much as anyone," Arthur said. "You all know the reason why. But how can we defeat him when he has such incredible powers?"

"Because he also has weaknesses," the Professor answered, "weaknesses and eccentricities. He cannot enter a strange place unless invited, or unless he has already sucked the blood of someone inside. He cannot pass through any door or window which has been sealed with garlic. He cowers and cringes at the sight of a crucifix. And perhaps his greatest weakness is that his powers only work at night. In daylight his form is fixed, so he prefers to be in the darkness of his tomb."

He frowned in concentration then turned to face Jonathan. "Your journal tells us about the boxes of earth which Dracula has had brought here. They came by ship. They are his resting places. It's a pity we don't know how many there are, but —"

"Fifty," Mina said. "It was in *The Whitby Times*."

"Excellent!" the Professor cried. "They were to be delivered to Carfax, a ruin in England that you found for him. Can you recall where this place is, Jonathan?"

"Of course. And I think you'll be surprised when you know," he said, smiling.

"It won't surprise me," Jack said. "I even saw the boxes being delivered!"

"Can you explain what you two talking about?" Arthur asked.

"Carfax is next door," Jonathan said.

"This hospital lies in its grounds," added Jack.

"Sometimes we depend more on luck than logic," the Professor said quietly.

There was a pause in the discussion. Perhaps all of them were thinking about Dracula, sated with blood, sleeping in one of his boxes not half a mile away.

"We'll go tonight," declared the Professor suddenly, "when Dracula probably isn't there."

"But. . . why?" Arthur asked.

"One of the things I have learned is that a vampire's lair can be sterilized with Holy Water. We'll sprinkle Holy Water in all fifty boxes. Then he'll have no resting place, and in the daylight, when his form is fixed, we'll hunt him down."

"But what if he's there?" Mina asked.

"If Dracula is asleep in one of his boxes, then. . . Well, we know what to do."

They began to discuss what time they should go to Carfax, and what weapons and equipment to take.

"Professor, one thing worries me," Mina said.

"What's that?"

"If we all of us go to Carfax, and – God forbid – we fail. . ."

"We won't fail," Jonathan muttered.

"We can't," said Arthur.

"But if we do, and we become. . . become like poor Lucy was, one of the Undead, then Dracula will be free to continue his evil work, and there'll be no one to resist him. You see, Professor, we're the only people in England who know about him. And who else would believe us if we told them?"

"She's right," Jack said quietly, after a few seconds thought.

"One of us has to stay behind," Mina continued, "and if the worst comes to the worst and the others fail to return, somehow that person will have to begin this dreadful fight all over again."

"It's a big responsibility," Jack said.

"I'll do it," Jonathan quickly volunteered.

"No, I'll do it," Arthur said.

"No, I'll do it," exclaimed Jack.

They began to argue, each one wanting to save the other from the possibility of facing Dracula alone.

"I think it should be me," Mina said calmly. "Dracula killed Lucy, my dearest, my oldest friend. He nearly killed my husband, the one person I love more than anyone. I hate this monster, and I want to see him dead. I know I have the courage and the stamina to face him alone if I have to. I know I can do it."

"Well let me stay behind too," Jonathan begged her.

"No. You must go to Carfax. You must not underestimate the difficulty of your task. There are a lot of boxes to sterilize. Every spare hand is needed."

Jonathan looked in despair at the Professor, as though appealing for him to intervene.

"Mina has decided," said the Professor simply.

They all fell silent. The men were thinking about Dracula, about destroying his sanctuary and – maybe

– killing him. But if they failed, if they died in the attempt, then it would be all down to Mina. She would have to be as clever as the Professor, as thoughtful as Jack, as brave as Jonathan, and as committed as Arthur. She would have to defeat Dracula alone.

Carfax

"Take these — and these, and these," the Professor directed, handing out crucifixes, garlic flowers, bottles of Holy Water, and a long, sharply-tipped stake.

They were standing next to the ominous stone stump of Carfax. It towered above them, a crumbling heap, Dracula's hiding place. From beneath its forbidding walls Jonathan looked back to the hospital, noticing some flickering lights through the trees. He couldn't help being glad that, for one night at least, Mina was safe. Then he turned to the others.

"I'll lead," he said. "Don't forget I've been here once before — when I was looking for a house for Dracula." He took them around the building, past the big front door, to a back wing where a smaller door was hanging from broken hinges.

"*In manus tuas, Domine!*" the Professor said — "*We are in your hands, Lord!*" — and they crossed the threshold. With grim purpose they walked in single file from one dark, filthy room to another, on the look-out for a desecrated chapel. After several wrong turns, Jonathan stopped in front of a low, arched door.

"This is the place."

"There's a funny smell here," Jack whispered, and

wrinkled his nose. Arthur placed his hands against the door and shoved. At first nothing happened as he strained and heaved. Then there was a sharp snap. The rusty iron hinges broke, and he fell inside.

Only Jonathan recognized the foul stench that assaulted their noses. It was as though Dracula's every vile breath was clinging to the place. Arthur, crouched on the floor, gagged and spluttered. The others stepped back, putting their hands over their noses.

"We can't go in there," Jack coughed.

"We haven't any choice," the Professor replied, entering the chapel.

Arthur got to his feet and with lamp in hand, moved farther in.

"Professor – the boxes!"

"Be careful," the Professor warned, his grip on the stake tightening. "He may be on the streets of London, pursuing his foul ways. But on the other hand. . ."

"Wherever he is," Arthur said, "he is about to become homeless."

He wedged his knife under the lid of a box and began to lever it off. The Professor handed Jonathan the stake and a heavy hammer and got out a bottle of Holy Water. Jonathan held his breath. He wanted Dracula to be in the box. He wanted to drive a stake through the detestable monster's heart.

"Ready?" Arthur hissed.

The other two nodded. Arthur raised the lid, revealing a great mound of Transylvanian soil. The Professor sprinkled a few drops of Holy Water on it.

"Now the evil is sterilized and Dracula cannot rest here," he said. "One down, forty-nine to go."

"I'm afraid not, Professor," said Jack, stepping up to them. "I've had a quick look around. There are only twenty-nine boxes here. And I found this receipt from a delivery firm." He held up a tattered piece of paper on which was written:

> Sir,
> Delivered as rekwested to a adress in
> London — 21 boxes of erth.
> Yours faythfully,
> Thomas Snelling, Snelling & Co.
>
> P.S. You hav a problem with your dranes.

"Blast!" Arthur exclaimed.

"Try not to get too impatient or angry," the

Professor cautioned him. "It's true that twenty-one boxes aren't here. But twenty-nine boxes *are* here, and if we sterilize them, then our job is more than half done."

"You're right," Arthur said. "Let's get to work."

After the men had set out for Carfax, Mina buried her nose in one of the Professor's old books. She wanted to keep herself busy so she wouldn't worry about Jonathan. And she needed to know as much as possible about the enemy in case it became her duty to defeat him. Her eyes grew wide as she read about an outbreak of vampirism a few centuries earlier:

> *The ancient townsfolk always knew when a vampire was stalking its prey. In the dead of night, every dog in the village would start howling at the moon. . .*

There seemed to be a lot of dogs barking *that* night. She listened for a few moments, wondering. Then she shook her head, and forced herself to go back to her book:

> *It was a time when people went out of their wits, when the sane became mad, and the mad became sane. . .*

Mina smiled to herself. The hospital was full of mad people, and none of them was showing any sudden signs of sanity! She closed her eyes, listening to the barking dogs and the noises of the night. It was then that she heard one of the patients chanting a strange rhyme:

> *"Where they go, he will leave,*
> *Where they leave, he will go.*
> *In the future they will grieve.*
> *Now prepare for blood to flow."*

It gave Mina the creeps. She snapped her book shut and decided to go to bed. What she needed was a good night's sleep.

Over at Carfax, the men were systematically sterilizing boxes. They were halfway through, and had become a bit too confident.

"Saw a rat just then," Jonathan observed, as he wrenched the lid from the fourteenth box.

"Huge rat over there," Arthur said, sprinkling Holy Water into the nineteenth box.

"Masses of them here," Jack said a little later, just as he was sealing box number twenty-seven. All four men glanced up from their work and looked around the room. Rats were appearing from nowhere, scuttling and scrabbling across the chapel floor, leaping over their feet, squeaking horribly.

"We must finish this task!" the Professor shouted, looking down in horror at the ocean of vermin around them.

Arthur desperately levered the lid from the twenty-eighth box as his feet entirely disappeared under rats.

"Sterilize it!" he shouted to Jack.

Jack needed no encouraging, quickly sprinkling it with Holy Water as a hundred rats clambered up his ankles. He looked across to Jonathan and the Professor. They were dealing with the last box, but the rats were deeper than ever.

"Come on!" he shouted to Arthur, and they pulled each other through the squealing, writhing mass to the safety of the door.

By the time the last box had been made safe, the

rats were at knee-level. Jonathan looked wildly around him – unless they could get out soon, they were going to drown in rats! He and the Professor started to wade through them.

"I can't make it!" the Professor cried. "Go on without me, carry on the battle! They're too deep!"

"We'll never do it without you!" Jonathan shouted, and he picked him up, slinging him over his shoulder.

"Put me down!" ordered the Professor.

Jonathan ignored him. He could feel the sinewy bodies of rats squirming against his legs as he forced a way through.

"They're huge!" he cried.

"*Rattus rattus maximus,*" called the Professor, "an interesting species. It's a direct descendant of the black rat, the rodent which spread the bubonic plague across Asia and Europe in the Middle Ages. It's absolutely fascinating to think how. . ."

"Shut up!" Jonathan shouted, desperately trying to pull his legs free.

"Hurry!" Arthur called from the chapel door. Jonathan made a last, frantic lunge, and just managed to get the Professor safely into Arthur's waiting hands. But in the attempt he fell over.

Immediately rats were clambering all over him, and in less than a second he was almost totally submerged. He felt as if he was being trampled to death. There were rats clawing at his face, squealing in his ears, scrabbling across his body. He tried to

fight his way out, but felt himself sink deeper and deeper. The rats pressed down on him so hard that it became difficult to breathe. Jonathan thought he was going to die. At that moment, he felt strong arms grab his collar. Jack was heaving him out.

"Mina would never forgive me if I let you drown in rats," he said.

Mina didn't stir when the exhausted Jonathan returned from Carfax. She was breathing in long, drawn out sighs, her hands opening and clenching like a sleeping baby's. She was in the middle of a dream about a white mist. It came creeping up to the hospital, low like a snake, and pressed itself against the walls and windows. Then it seeped into her room through a narrow gap and. . .

Jonathan looked down at her. He was pleased she was sleeping so soundly. The horrific escapade with the rats had amply illustrated Dracula's powers. They nearly hadn't made it. So Mina needed all the sleep she could get, just in case the rest of them didn't survive.

In the morning, as he was telling her about the night's events, he noticed she didn't look very well.

"I think I must be coming down with something," Mina admitted. "I feel so tired and weak."

"I was going to ask you to help me find the other boxes, but perhaps you should stay here instead."

"I think I ought to stay in bed today," Mina agreed.

It took Jonathan only twenty minutes to find Snelling and Co., less than five minutes to track down Thomas Snelling, and the rest of the day to extract the information he needed. It wasn't that Thomas Snelling couldn't *remember* where he had delivered the other boxes. As he told Jonathan again and again, in great detail and at enormous length, he *could*. And it wasn't as if he didn't *want* to tell Jonathan where he had delivered the other boxes. As became completely clear during the course of a long and tedious monologue, he *did*.

"Well just tell me then," pleaded Jonathan. "It really is vitally important."

"Can't do it," Thomas Snelling said, shaking his head gloomily. "I only wish I could, but I can't."

"But why?"

"On account of my illness, which makes talking difficult."

Jonathan stared in disbelief.

"But you've been talking to me for ages! In fact you've been talking to me for ages, and you haven't even said anything yet!"

"Exactly," Thomas Snelling said, shaking his head gravely at the tragedy of his condition. "That's what's so difficult about it. That is the nature of my terrible ailment."

"Are you seriously telling me that you suffer from a medical condition which prevents you from saying things when you talk?"

"That's it – that's it in a nutshell. And there's only one known cure."

"What is it?"

"Now you might find this hard to believe," Thomas Snelling warned.

"Go on."

"But all the most respected medical authorities have reached the same conclusion."

"Just get on with it!"

"The *suffering* I had to endure before the cure was found," he said, shuddering at the memory, "the pain, the agony, the. . ."

"What is the cure?" Jonathan said through gritted teeth, resisting the urge to swear. Thomas Snelling leaned back in his chair, shook his head sadly, and scratched his chin.

"Bodkin's Best Bitter," he sighed.

They went to The Bull's Head, The Trafalgar, The Joiner's Inn, The Speckled Pigeon, The Duke of York, The Three Kings, The Ramsden Croft, The Little Fella, The Billy Boy, The Varsity Tavern, The Prince of Wales and The Frisky Ferret.

"I'm starting to feel a conslidrabbable improvement," Mr. Snelling declared, beaming broadly.

"It's amazing what modern medical science can achieve," Jonathan said drily.

"One more dose should do it," said Snelling. "The full and glorious powers of speech are beginning to vein through my courses."

"I beg your pardon?"

"Er, course through my veins."

It was in The Ribald Rabbit, just before midnight, after a few more restorative measures of Bodkin's Best Bitter, that Thomas Snelling felt sufficiently recovered to tell Jonathan where he had delivered the boxes.

"Number nine," he breathed. "Number nine, Piccadi-pippadi-dilly."

"Number nine Piccadilly?"

"Stank like a *hic!* – stank like a *hic!* – like a *hic!* – oh, never mind," and he slumped beneath the table and fell asleep.

Jonathan rushed back to the others at the hospital. They could go to Piccadilly right away and sterilize the remaining boxes.

"What took you so long?" Arthur exclaimed.

"Don't ask. I know where the other boxes are. I'll just go and see how Mina is, then let's go.

"Hurry!" Arthur implored him.

As they waited for him to return, one of the hospital nurses ran into the room.

"Doctor Seward," he cried, "one of the patients has had a terrible accident! You must come quickly!"

"I can't," Jack said, "I'm too busy. I can't explain now. You'll have to deal with it yourself."

The nurse threw his hands up in despair.

"But there's blood all over the place, and he's moaning and crying. He says he must see you because of the vampire, and I'm too scared to. . ."

"Because of the what?" Jack interrupted sharply.

"Because of the vampire."

"Which patient is it?"

"Renfield."

Jack looked at the Professor.

"What's going on?" he asked.

"There's only one way to find out," the Professor answered, grimly.

They found Renfield lying in a glittering pool of blood. His injuries were horrible, and there was blood and broken furniture everywhere as though he had been thrown around the room by a terrible force. There was no doubt that he was dying. But when he saw Jack crouch down next to him, he began to breathe harder, and his mouth opened.

"He said he would make me sane," Renfield whispered, "so that I could go free. He promised."

"Who did?" the Professor asked.

"He kept coming to the bars of my window," Renfield continued. "He said he would make me sane if I did what he said."

"Who?" Jack said. "Who was it?"

"He broke his promise!" Renfield cried. "I did what he asked, but he came in a white mist and turned into a great wolf, shaking me in his jaws like a rabbit!"

"Dracula. . ." Jack hissed, closing his eyes.

"I called him Lord and Master!" Renfield moaned, "I invited him inside! Forgive me!"

A glassy look came over his eyes, his head turned to one side, and he died.

The three men looked at each other, speechless with shock. Arthur was the first to break the silence.

"Mina!" he shouted.

As they rushed to the Harkers' bedroom, the same image haunted each of them. It was an image of Dracula bending down over Mina's throat; of his bloody fangs piercing her skin. Perhaps for those few moments they were lucky. Because the truth was harder to bear.

Outside the bedroom door they paused briefly. The Professor tried the handle, pressing it slowly and silently down. The door was locked. He gestured to Arthur to kick it open. Arthur took a step back, summoned all his strength, and gave the door an almighty kick. It flew open, smashing into the inside wall with a loud bang, to reveal the unbearable scene within.

Moonlight was flooding the room, illuminating a spectacle so shocking that the hairs on the back of Jack's neck rose.

"Oh Mina. . ." he whispered.

For a few moments they were all incapable of action. They could only watch in fascinated horror.

Inside the room, under an open window, Jonathan was lying on the floor in a stupor. A huge red mark on his cheek indicated that he had been felled by a savage blow. As for Mina, the tell-tale wounds on her neck showed that Dracula had been feasting on her blood. And now he was standing above her, dark and merciless, utterly absorbed in his evil deed. He had pulled open his shirt and gouged a long cut in his chest with his fingernails. He had dripped blood onto Mina's forehead so that it trickled down her face.

"Monster!" Arthur suddenly yelled, breaking the trance. Dracula rotated his head slowly to face them, an indescribable look of disdain and contempt etched into his features. His eyes were flaming red with fury, and his nostrils quivered and flared. His teeth, stained with blood, were champing together like those of a wild beast. Then he sprang at them. But in that instant the Professor held out a crucifix. Dracula came to a halt as though hitting a brick wall. He stared at the small cross, cowering and cringing before it, then looked at the Professor in bewilderment.

"We've got him now," Arthur hissed triumphantly.

He held out his own crucifix, and Jack did the same. They began to advance. Dracula moved backward to the window, step by step, as delicately as a cat. For a split second he smiled, exhibiting his gore-stained teeth. Then, before their eyes, he faded into countless specks which formed a cloud and wafted out of the window. Jack ran to the window and looked out. A great black bat was flapping westward.

From the bed came a scream so ear-piercing, so heart-rending, so full of despair, that they would never forget it. Mina was sitting up, rocking to and fro, her eyes wild with terror. As if responding to his wife, Jonathan began to wake up, moaning in agony on the floor. He felt at the wound on his face. Then he looked up, not seeming to know where he was or what had happened. But a second chilling scream from Mina told him.

"Unclean!" Mina wailed, desperately rubbing the blood off her face with the bedclothes. Jonathan rushed to her. The others could do nothing but witness the agony and the suffering.

"He drank my blood," sobbed Mina, "and stained me with his own!" The Professor stepped forward and lifted Mina's head with his hand.

"I will touch your forehead with the cross. In the name of the Father, the Son and the Holy —"

It seemed impossible that things could get worse. But as he pressed the cross on Mina's forehead she cried out in pain, and it seared into her flesh as if it were made from white-hot metal, to leave an ugly red welt. The Professor, for the first time in many years, began to cry.

"What else?" he shouted into the night. "What next?"

It was Jonathan who replied.

"Don't give up now, Professor," he said. "If you give up, we all will. And how can we do that, when Mina is in danger of. . . of being a. . ."

"Say it," Mina whispered.

But Jonathan couldn't, shaking his head miserably.

"Then I will instead," Mina said resolutely; "a vampire!" Her husband nodded, hatred for Dracula making him grind his teeth together.

"Tonight," Mina said, "there is no time for anything but grief and horror. But when the morning comes," she said bravely, "then we must start again."

The Vampire Vanishes

The house at Number Nine Piccadilly was not like Carfax, where they could enter at will without anyone seeing. It was at the very heart of a bustling city street where all manner of traders and hawkers were busily peddling their wares, and horses and carriages were clattering up and down.

"We'll have to break in," the Professor decided.

"But the street is *seething* with people," Jack said, "and I can see at least two policemen."

"Has anyone got a better idea?" A marked silence revealed that no one had. "Wait here," the Professor told them, walking away without explanation.

They found a bench to sit on opposite the house. It was a large town house, rather shabby, with shutters over the windows. It looked out of place among the elegant properties nearby, with their gleaming front doors and open windows.

"What is he *doing?*" Jonathan fumed after fifteen minutes had passed. The events of the previous evening had made him desperate to confront Dracula. Every wasted moment meant Mina became closer to being a vampire.

"I think something must have gone wrong,"

Arthur said eventually. "We'll have to –"

"Look!" Jack interrupted.

A carriage was pulling up outside the house. The Professor got out of the vehicle in a leisurely way and paid the driver. Another man got out of the carriage too, yawning wearily and scratching his not inconsiderable belly.

"Who's that?" Jonathan asked.

The old Professor laughed loudly at a joke made by the carriage driver. Then he turned to his companion, who was carrying a basket of tools, and said a few words.

"It's a locksmith," Arthur said. "They're going to break in, bold as you like, under everyone's noses!"

As the locksmith worked, the Professor sat on a wall and read about the cricket in *The Times*. No one took a scrap of notice of him until a policeman sauntered up and tapped him on the shoulder.

"Oh no," Jack muttered.

The constable and the Professor started to have a heated discussion.

"We're finished," Jonathan groaned. "Why didn't we stop him? Come on." He jumped up from the bench and walked over to the house. The others followed.

The policeman began to go red in the face, gesturing furiously as he explained something, and the Professor became equally animated in his response. While they were still arguing, the locksmith turned the handle of the front door and pushed it open.

"Ah, splendid!" the Professor declared, just as Arthur and the others came up to them.

"Well, it's been a great pleasure talking to you, sir," the policeman said, "even though you know less about cricket than just about any man I ever met. Why, W.G. Grace is the finest batsman in England!"

"The pleasure was all mine, constable, I assure you," the Professor replied with a smile, "although it pains me to say that your understanding of spin bowling seems to be less than adequate." He suddenly saw his friends watching them in bewilderment. "Arthur! Jonathan! And Jack! What a surprise! You can be the first to see my new house!"

"Er," said Arthur, "yes. How lovely."

"Well sir, good day to you," said the policeman as he walked away.

"And to you," said the Professor, waving cheerily. He paid the locksmith, led the others inside, and shut the heavy door.

"We thought you'd been caught," said Jonathan, amazed at his coolness.

"You underestimate me," the Professor answered. He sniffed the air, his brow puckering. "The next thing to do is find the source of that horrible smell."

They explored the house, sticking together in case Dracula was already there. It was a gloomy old place, damp and empty, and it looked like no one had lived in it for years. Upstairs there was no smell at all, but they searched each room anyway. Downstairs there was an awful stink, and when they went into the dining room, where the stench was so disgusting that it nearly knocked them over, they found what they were looking for. Numerous boxes were stacked up at one end of the room.

"It looks like they're all here!" Arthur exclaimed, quickly counting them: "fifteen, sixteen, seventeen, eighteen. . ."

"At last," Jonathan whispered.

". . . nineteen, twenty. . . Blast!"

There was one box missing. Jonathan and Arthur looked at the Professor in despair. He was carefully placing the contents of his bag on the floor.

"He has another hiding place," he said briskly, "but if we kill him today, what does it matter?"

"I hope he doesn't try that rat trick again," Jack said as they prepared to sterilize the boxes.

"He won't," the Professor said. "His vile powers can only work in darkness, although in the daylight he will still be strong and deadly."

Because it was daytime, it was far more likely that Dracula would be inside one of the boxes than had been the case at Carfax. They sterilized each box with great care, Jack and Jonathan levering off the lid, the Professor sprinkling in Holy Water, and Arthur standing near, holding a stake and a hammer ready. The tension grew with every box they treated. After they had found that the nineteenth box had nothing but soil in it, they prepared themselves for the last one. It was at the very back of the room, slightly apart from the others. It somehow seemed more than likely that Dracula would be in it.

"Go on," Arthur urged, as Jack and Jonathan struggled to open it.

"This lid's a lot tighter than the others," Jack panted, pulling at it with all his strength.

"Get ready," the Professor whispered to Arthur. "Don't stop to think, just do it."

Arthur gripped the stake tightly in his left hand and raised the hammer in his right. There was the sound of wood splintering, then the lid burst open, and in his eagerness Arthur almost fell inside. The only thing in the box was earth.

"Well, well," the Professor mused solemnly.

"Now what?" Arthur asked, straightening up.

"Now we get our weapons ready, and we wait."

Jonathan clenched his hands into fists. His weary face seemed older than his years. How could he wait when Mina was facing a fate worse than death?

"What if he doesn't come?" he asked the Professor in a quiet voice.

"He will," the Professor said. "Although he may suspect we've sterilized the boxes, he won't know for sure until he actually sees for himself. Also," he continued, getting so wrapped up in his own explanation that he forgot about Jonathan's feelings, "he feasted well last night, so he will want to sleep."

He feasted well last night. . . the words tortured Jonathan, searing into his mind as painfully as the crucifix had seared into Mina's skin. Dracula had to be stopped! If they got the chance today, they had to succeed! Just as he was thinking this, he heard a noise. A key was slowly turning in the lock of the front door.

For a moment, they all stood stock-still, looking at each other. Then, without a sound, they positioned themselves around the room. They heard the front door being carefully opened, and the soft tread of Dracula in the hall. He was creeping nearer to them as slowly and as stealthily as a cat stalking a mouse. He seemed to stop just outside the door of the room.

Silence fell. It probably only lasted half a minute, but to the men inside the room, it felt like a week. Jonathan tightened his grip on the dagger he was holding. Every muscle in his body strained for action. He willed the dining room door to open, slowly, so that he could plunge the deadly blade into Dracula's chest. He had never felt more alert, more prepared, more –

BANG! The door burst open, and even as it slammed back into the wall Dracula was already in the middle of the room. He had sprung in with a single bound, so swift and agile that no one even had a chance to stop him. There had been something so panther-like in the vampire's movement, so inhuman, that they were all – even Jonathan – too shocked to move.

Dracula circled warily in the middle of the room. His hands were held out like claws, ready to swipe and slash. He snarled like a wild beast, savage and blood-thirsty. They knew he had none of his nocturnal powers, but he seemed more dangerous than ever, like a maddened animal in a trap.

The four men began to advance on him. Jack and the Professor were holding out their crucifixes, while Jonathan had his dagger raised above his head, and Arthur carried a hammer and a wooden stake, its tip sharpened to a deadly point. Dracula hissed and spat at them. The monstrous expression of loathing and fury on his face terrified his attackers, but they closed in on him relentlessly, so that there seemed to be no way he could escape.

Jonathan suddenly lunged forward, bringing his dagger down as hard as he could. He moved quickly and used all his strength, but Dracula was even quicker, side-stepping the blow so that the blade ripped through his clothes instead of his heart. From the rip in his cloak, dozens of gold coins came spilling out, bouncing on the floor and rolling into the corners of the room.

Jonathan stepped back, his eyes holding Dracula's gaze, his every thought intent on killing the vampire. The other three moved even closer in, trapping Dracula in a smaller circle. Jack's crucifix was so near the vampire's ghastly white face that he flinched with terror. Seeing his chance, Jonathan lunged again.

Dracula ducked with super-human speed to avoid the blow, then dived from beneath Jonathan's arm and out of the circle, rolling over once and springing to his feet. Arthur and Jack dived after him, but he was so fast that it was as if they were moving in slow motion. The vampire grabbed a handful of gold coins from the floor and then, with a single leap, threw himself at the window. There was an ear-splitting crash as the glass shattered into countless shards and splinters. He tumbled into the cobbled courtyard at the back of the house, springing up unharmed, then turned to face his attackers, who had run to the window.

"You think you can defeat me," he snarled, "but I am Dracula, Prince of Darkness, Lord of the Undead! I can never be defeated! I have time, more time than you can imagine. My reign will last for ten thousand years! I'll be sucking the blood of your children's children when each and every one of you is rotting in the grave!" Then he turned and fled, vaulting easily over a high brick wall.

The three younger men scrambled out of the window. Jack was first into the courtyard, and he ran to the wall and tried to climb it. Arthur ran up behind him and pushed him up. On top of the wall, Jack looked left and right onto a busy street. There was no sign of Dracula.

Jack slithered back down the wall, shaking his

head. The Professor joined them, having clambered down clumsily from the dining room window.

"Let us not despair," he said quietly. "He had fifty hiding places, and now he has only one."

"Yes," said Jonathan bitterly, "but he might choose to hide in it for a hundred years."

Back at the hospital Mina was waiting. She bowed her head when the Professor described how Dracula had escaped, knowing that her soul was still in peril. They decided to have a meeting, racking their brains about what to do next. But what could they do? They had nothing to go on. The house in Piccadilly had contained no clue, so Dracula's last box could be anywhere in London.

"As we can't hope to find him," Mina said after a long silence, "we have to hope he will find us again."

"What do you mean?" Jack asked.

"I mean that our only hope is that he will come back and. . . and try to. . . try to. . ."

"And try to what?" Jonathan asked gently.

"To suck my blood again," Mina answered flatly.

"What a terrible thing to hope for," Jack whispered.

"We have to make it easy for him," Mina said. "There must be no garlic rubbed around the windows. There must be no —"

"How can you suggest such a thing!" Jonathan cried. "How can you expect me to just let him waltz in and attack you?"

"But we have no choice!" Mina replied. "If he can't attack *me*, how can we attack *him*? And Jonathan, what have I got to lose?"

Jonathan looked at her. The red cross on her forehead, which looked so raw and painful, was the terrible proof that she was right.

It was a gloomy group of friends who prepared for the night ahead. Once Mina and Jonathan were in bed, Jack and the Professor hid themselves in the little boxroom which adjoined the bedroom, and Arthur positioned himself outside in the corridor.

The wait was long and fruitless. Each second crawled past like a minute, and each minute crawled past like an hour. No wind rustled the leaves of the trees; the night was silent, utterly silent. And when four o'clock became five o'clock, the Professor knew Dracula wouldn't come. Already the blackness of the night was beginning to lift. He led Jack out of the boxroom, and called for Arthur.

"I'm sorry," he said simply, "but he won't come now. Perhaps if we try again tomorrow night. And yet. . ." he sighed. "My fear, my great fear, is that Dracula will not come here again. As he boasted to us, time is on his side, and —"

"Professor," Mina interrupted him, sitting up in bed with a strange look in her eyes, "Professor, you must hypnotize me!"

Professor Van Helsing was so surprised by this sudden request that he didn't know what to say.

"Quickly!" Mina told him, "before the night has gone, but before the day is here. I don't know why, but you must hypnotize me!"

Doing as she said, he sat on the edge of the bed and started to swing his big old pocket watch slowly in front of her face. Mina's eyes followed the gentle motion. After a few minutes her breathing became slow regular and slow, and her eyes closed. She was in a trance. The four men watched her, fascinated, wondering what she was going to say.

"Who are you?" the Professor whispered.

"I am not me," Mina answered slowly in a low, dreamy voice.

"Where are you?"

"I do not know."

"What can you see?"

"Nothing."

"What are you doing?"

"Nothing."

The Professor sighed and looked up at the others, then turned back to Mina.

"What can you hear?" he asked, with little hope.

"I hear the sound of water. It is lapping at the hull."

"You are on a ship?"

"Yes."

"What else can you hear?"

"The shouting of orders. The flapping of the sails."

"What do you feel like?" the Professor asked.

"Like I am dead, but I am not."

"Then you are alive?"

"I am neither alive nor dead."

By this time the sun had almost risen. Mina became restless in her trance, her head moving from side to side and her eyelids quivering.

"Where are you?" the Professor asked again urgently.

Mina's eyes opened and she looked up at all of them.

"Was I talking in my sleep?" she asked.

"No," the Professor said gently, looking at her. "I'm afraid Dracula was."

After a stunned silence, they all started to bombard him with questions.

"I don't understand it myself," he said, raising a hand to silence them. "The dawn seems to be a critical time for vampires. Just as a vampire is neither alive nor dead, the dawn is neither the night nor the day. Somehow Mina has been able to access the monster's mind. Dawn has always been a time of mystery and fascination, a symbol of death and renewal, a subject for great art. The Ancient Greeks wrote poems about the dawn. And the Romans. In fact, if I'm not mistaken, I think you'll find that the Provençal poets of twelfth-century France had a category of poem called *Alba* – derived from the Latin for white, *albus* – in which they. . ."

While he talked, he started to polish his shoes

with his handkerchief, a sure sign that he was going to talk about something really boring for a very long time.

"Never mind all that now," Jonathan said brusquely. "This is our lucky break. He's on a ship. We've got to find him."

"That's why he picked up the money in the Piccadilly House!" Arthur exclaimed. "He needed it so that he could get home!"

"He is frightened of us!" the Professor declared with a broad grin. "He has taken his one box and he is trying to escape to Transylvania, and the safety of his castle!"

"He won't succeed," Jonathan vowed. "Even if we have to chase him right up to the front door of that miserable place, we'll stop him."

"That won't be necessary," the Professor said. "All we have to do is work out which ship he's on and which port it's going to. Then we can travel there by land, faster than he can, and wait for him."

After a quick breakfast, Arthur set off to visit Lloyds, the shipping organization. He had many contacts there, and was hoping that someone would be able to tell him about any recent sailings to Eastern Europe. The others stayed at home. Mina wanted to talk to Jonathan, and the Professor wanted to talk to Jack.

"What is it?" Jack asked, as his old friend led him into the study.

The Professor sighed, hesitating before he spoke.

"It's Mina," he said.

"What about her?"

"She's. . . changing."

A shiver ran down Jack's spine.

"I can see the fateful signs of the vampire coming into her face," the Professor continued. "It's very slight at the moment, but her eyes seem to be harder, and her teeth, if I'm not mistaken, appear to be sharper. And it seems to be a great effort for her to speak her mind. It's almost as if. . ."

"As if what?"

"As if there was a great battle going on within her, between good and bad, between what she was and what she will become. There will come a point," he said bluntly, "when she will be our enemy."

"Professor!" Jack whispered.

"It's the truth," his friend said, shrugging, "however unpalatable we may find it. But the thing is, I don't know what to do about it. If we take her with us she may, against her will, try to foil us. But if we leave her here, there'll be no one to. . ."

"To what?"

"To. . . release her," said the Professor tactfully, "from this curse – like Arthur did for Lucy."

Outside in the garden, Mina and Jonathan were pacing up and down.

"No!" Jonathan said, "I refuse to believe it!"

Mina put her fingers to her temples, as though speaking the truth actually hurt.

"Look at me Jonathan!" she implored him. "Look at my teeth!"

Jonathan could see only too well that her teeth were slightly longer and slightly sharper, but he didn't want to know.

"I am not a vampire yet," Mina whispered, "but I'm turning into one. And that's why I want you all to do something for me. . ."

At least when Arthur returned later that day, he brought some good news.

"Only one ship sailed to Eastern Europe yesterday," he informed them. "It's called the *Czarina Catherine*. It's going to Varna in Transylvania."

"Excellent!" Professor Van Helsing exclaimed.

"They're due to reach Varna in three weeks. If we cross the Channel tonight, then travel overland, we can be there in two."

They all began to discuss the best route, and what they would do when they arrived. All except Mina.

"Two weeks is a long time," she said quietly. She looked at each one of them in turn. "A lot can change in two weeks."

"I am glad you have raised this subject," the Professor said uneasily.

"I looked in the mirror today, Professor. Do you know what I saw?"

The Professor hesitated. Arthur put his arm around Jonathan, who had slumped against the wall.

"You saw that your teeth were longer," the

Professor said finally. Mina smiled at him sadly.

"Yes, I saw that my teeth were longer," she said, "but guess what else I saw?"

"I. . . I don't know," said the Professor. "It's true that your eyes can seem a little colder at times," he stammered, wincing as if it hurt him to say so.

"It's worse than that. I saw the clock on the wall."

"I don't understand," said the Professor flatly. "I could look in a mirror myself and see a clock on the wall. It all depends on the various physical laws of light and reflection. You see, the reflected ray of light lies in the same plane as the angle of incidence. Now, of course, some scientists think —"

"Professor, I saw the clock through my face."

"There was no reflection?" the Professor breathed in horror.

"No, I wasn't. . . I was there, but I wasn't there as well. I could see myself, but I could see through myself too." Her voice quavered a little, but she continued. "I know exactly what's happening to me, Professor, because I know what happened to dear Lucy. And it's my greatest fear that, as time passes, I will become a danger to the people I love."

"But —" Jonathan said.

"And it goes beyond just us," Mina continued. "God knows how much I love my husband and all of you, but the only thing that matters is the destruction of Dracula. That is why you have to make me a promise. You know what it is."

"Don't make me promise it," Jonathan begged.

"If the time comes," Mina said, "you must promise to kill me – to kill me in the way that we all know."

"You are a very, very brave woman," the Professor sighed. "And I. . . I solemnly swear to you that you have my promise."

"You have mine too," said Jack hoarsely.

"And mine," Arthur said.

Jonathan, blinking back his tears, could only nod.

The Deadly Chase

Mina, Jack, Arthur, Jonathan and the Professor left London in the morning, arriving in Paris the next night, where they reserved some seats on the Orient Express. The train sped through the night and reached Varna at five o'clock the next day. After they had found a hotel and unpacked, Arthur rushed off to the British Consulate. He had arranged for a telegram to be sent to Varna every day by Lloyds, telling him if the *Czarina Catherine* had been sighted. While he was gone, the others met in Mina and Jonathan's room. It was just before sunset.

"Are you ready?" the Professor asked Mina.

Mina nodded. He got out his old pocket watch and, holding it by the chain, he started to swing it to and fro in front of her eyes.

"What can you see?" he asked her, when she was fully hypnotized.

"Nothing. All is dark."

"What can you hear?"

"Waves lapping on the hull. . . Water rushing by, and the creaking of timbers."

"Where are you?"

Silence.

"At least we know he's still at sea," Jack said. "All we have to do now is wait."

"Wait!" Jonathan exclaimed bitterly. "I'm sick of waiting!"

"And Mina is sick *from* it," the Professor said sadly, scanning her sleeping face. The tips of two sharp teeth were protruding from her lips.

They had calculated that it would take up to two weeks for the ship to arrive, but in the end it took even longer. Every day Mina's teeth seemed fractionally larger, and her eyes slightly colder. She was starting to sleep in the day, and wake at night. And she spoke to them less and less.

"Seventeen days!" Jonathan groaned to Jack in the middle of the third week. "Seventeen days, when it should have taken fourteen, and not a word!"

"The ship must have hit bad weather," Jack suggested.

"That fiend can control the weather!" Jonathan exploded. But at that moment Arthur ran in with a telegram.

"The ship's arrived!" he cried. "But I'm afraid –"

"Thank God!" Jonathan said, and he snatched the piece of paper from Arthur's hand: *Czarina Catherine reported entering port of Galatz at nine o clock today.*

"Galatz?" Jonathan groaned. "Galatz? In God's name, where on earth is Galatz?"

"That's what I wanted to tell you," Arthur said. "Somehow he's tricked us. Galatz is miles away."

They spent the whole day on a train, mentally urging it to go faster as it hurtled the hundreds of miles to Galatz. As soon as they arrived they went to the port and tracked down the *Czarina Catherina*. The Captain was only too pleased to meet some English people, and he took them aboard.

"The strangest passage I ever made in my life," he told them. "London to the Black Sea with a bloomin' force four on a bloomin' beam reach and barely a bloomin' jibe or ready-about to shake a stick at."

"Oh dear," said the Professor sympathetically.

"Oh dear?" repeated the Captain. "Oh dear? It was the best bloomin' wind I ever had!"

"In that case," Jonathan asked angrily, "why did you arrive so late?"

"And in the wrong port," Arthur couldn't help pointing out.

The captain gave them a long, withering look.

"Done a lot of sailing, have you?" he asked.

"Er. . ." said Arthur.

"Ever been battered from bow to bridge by a breaker in the Bay of Biscay?"

"Er. . ." said Arthur.

"Or faced freezing to death in the fo'c'sle in a frigorific fog off the Faroes?"

"Er. . ." said Arthur.

"As you know so much about sailing, you'd know what to do when a fog settles on a boat like a leech and won't shift for love nor money."

"A fog?" asked the Professor, his eyebrows rising.

"That's it," said the Captain, nodding. "Sat on the boat for six days solid, so we had to drop anchor, and yet the wind never let up. Now what do you make of that, sir?"

"Interesting," said the Professor.

"Never known a good blow to leave a fog alone like that. Meanwhile the crew gets the bloomin' heebie-jeebies, chattering about this blasted box we had below. Half of 'em wanted to chuck it overboard, and the other half wanted to open it up, throw in a couple of old crosses and a big bunch of garlic flowers, seal it, and *then* chuck it overboard. Bloomin' lunatics."

"Were they Transylvanians?" the Professor asked.

"Most of 'em," the Captain told him. "Well I says to them that I wasn't having any funny business on my ship, but I could see they might turn nasty, and as we were running low on food and water anyway, I decided to set sail."

"In the fog?"

"In the fog, using just the jib. Well that shut 'em up. Sailing in a fog is scarier than some old box, as our young sailing expert here will doubtless confirm."

Arthur nodded in agreement, his face turning red.

"And then what happened?" the Professor asked intently.

"After a bit I decided to belay avast, but a big bruiser blew midships and gave us a cringle, broaching the boat abaft, and that was that."

"I'm afraid I don't quite. . . follow you," the Professor admitted.

"Bloomin' landlubber," the Captain muttered. "We was blown into this 'ere port, miles from Varna where we was headed. And then, before I even knew where we were, a load of bloomin' gypsies came on board. They wanted that box."

"But surely you didn't give it to them?" Jonathan asked.

"Certainly not!" said the Captain in a hurt and offended tone. "I run a tidy ship, I do. You see, I'm a skipper of the old school, a seafaring gent with my good reputation to keep, and I don't allow any old landlubbers to march straight onto my bloomin' vessel and take whatever they bloomin' well want whenever they bloomin' well feel like it."

"Thank God!" Jonathan cried, seizing him by the hand and shaking it gratefully.

"Well, as I say, I'm a skipper of the old school, and I run my ship accordingly. So I charged them fifty quid, and. . ."

"You did what?"

". . . and off they went with it."

Jonathan dropped the man's hand as though it were a red hot poker. "You charged them fifty pounds?" he repeated. "You idiot!"

"I thought you said you were a skipper of the old school," Arthur said, "with your good reputation to keep. What sort of Captain sells his cargo off for fifty pounds?"

"You think it wasn't enough?" the Captain asked. "You might be right. They were flush with cash. Still, fifty quid is always fifty quid, no matter what you say. You can buy a lot with fifty quid," and, so saying, he rolled up his trouser leg to reveal a brand new, highly polished wooden leg.

"It's mahogany," he informed them proudly.

"I can't stand it any more," Jonathan said back at the hotel. "Every time we think we've got him, he gets away. And Mina. . . she. . . I. . ." He put his head in his hands and tried to regain his composure. It was easy to see why he was so distressed. Mina seemed to be ever more distant, and he couldn't bear to think about that dreadful promise.

Mina suddenly sighed, long and loud. They all looked at her. She had hardly said anything for two days. She was screwing up her face and clenching her fists, almost as if she were in pain.

"Don't. . . give. . . up," she said, grimacing. "Hypnotize. . . again," she managed, then sank back into her chair.

"Mina!" Jonathan exclaimed, rushing to her side.

"She's fighting an extraordinary battle," the Professor muttered as he fumbled for his watch. "It's sheer willpower that has stopped her from becoming a vampire already."

Once more the Professor put Mina under hypnosis and asked her what she could see.

"Darkness," she answered.

"What can you hear?"

"Water lapping on the hull, and the sound of –"

"He's still on the ship!" Arthur whispered in astonishment. "The Captain lied to us, he –"

"Silence!" the Professor ordered. Mina shifted uneasily.

"Where are you?" he asked. She groaned, and her hands gripped the sides of her chair.

"Where are you?" he said again.

Mina's mouth opened and closed. Her forehead was covered in sweat. Her breaths were coming in great, heaving gasps.

"Sereth!" she shouted, making them all jump. Then she fell into a deep sleep.

"There's no such place as Sereth," Arthur said, springing up, "but it doesn't matter because he's obviously still on that ship. The sooner we get back there, the better."

"It's true that there's no such place as Sereth," the Professor agreed. "But that's because Sereth is a river. It winds its way through deepest Transylvania, right to the Borgo Pass. He's on a riverboat."

They decided to pursue Dracula by horse.

"We'll never catch up in another boat," Arthur said, "but if we follow him up the riverbank, we're bound to get him."

"I'll travel directly to Castle Dracula," the Professor said, "and render it. . . uninhabitable for vampires, shall we say, just in case you don't succeed."

"And Mina?" Jonathan asked.

"She must come with me," the Professor said.

Jonathan's jaw dropped open.

"Do you mean to say that you would take Mina into the very jaws of that evil place?"

"But you don't understand —"

"No, *you* don't understand what that place is like, where every speck of dust is a monster, and even the moonlight is alive with vampires! Mina must not go there! She'll be safer with me."

The Professor shook his head. "I wish you were right," he said, "and I wish I didn't have to point out this simple fact."

"What simple fact?"

"That if you catch up with Dracula before he gets to the castle, and try to kill him, Mina would be a great hindrance."

"Why?"

The Professor took a deep breath before he answered.

"Because she may be on his side."

"Professor!" Arthur shouted, "Mina would never do such a thing."

"No," the Professor said, "Mina wouldn't. But who knows if she'll still be Mina tomorrow, or the day after?"

At first light next day, on the bank of the River Sereth, the two parties went their separate ways. The Professor helped Mina into their carriage. Jack, on a magnificent chestnut stallion, waved his hat to them, then galloped away. Jonathan remained motionless on his own horse. He was looking at Mina's face framed in the carriage window, and wondering if he would ever see her again. Then Arthur called to him, and together they chased after Jack.

All day long the Professor and Mina raced through the countryside, stopping only to change their horses. The next day, the country they rode through was noticeably wilder. The mountains enclosed them as though they were in a great rocky prison. The Professor expected to reach Castle Dracula by sunset. With every passing minute he could feel his anxiety building. It wasn't eased by the change coming over Mina, who seemed to be losing the awful battle raging within her. She was starting to smile in a disturbing way, looking eagerly to the most distant crags as though she were going home. And when he had tried to hypnotize her just before dawn, she had refused to answer.

It was at about four in the afternoon that the Professor halted the horses. There, ahead of them, was Castle Dracula, perched on the top of a mountain like an enormous raven ready to swoop, dark and ominous. A long, winding track led up to it, with dense forest encroaching on either side.

"We're here," he called loudly, jumping down and opening her door.

From inside, like a wolf in a cage, Mina watched him. A half-smile quivered on her lips, a smile of cunning and contempt. Her eyes flashed with sudden fury. The mark on her forehead was more lurid than ever, only now it seemed more like a badge of identity than a tragic scar.

"We're here," the Professor repeated in a quiet voice. "You must hang on, Mina, for one more day – please. Do you understand?"

Mina said nothing. Professor Van Helsing put his hands over his face in despair. The time had come. Mina herself had extracted the fateful promise from him – the promise to kill her. For the sake of her soul, and for all humanity, it had to be done. As he stared into her eyes, he tried not to remember how she had once been. He told himself that he was a scientist, a man of reason and logic, who had never shirked a plain fact in his life, no matter how painful. And the plain fact was this: she was a vampire.

"Forgive me," he whispered in a broken voice.

He shut the door and turned away to get the stake and hammer. There was a noise from inside the carriage and he looked back to see Mina pressing her face to the window, and sliding her hands down the glass. On her face was such an expression of anguish and turmoil that he cried out in alarm. She was mouthing something. He couldn't hear it, but he could tell what it was: "Jonathan."

He rushed back to her and opened the door.

"We'll risk another day," he whispered, holding the crucifix in his pocket with one hand and helping her down from the carriage with the other. He led her to a clearing where he intended to set up camp. The first thing he did, even before he fed and watered the horses, was to scratch a ring in the earth around Mina. Snow started to fall as he sprinkled it with Holy Water and pressed garlic flowers into the soil. Mina watched him listlessly, snowflakes spotting her clothes. At one point, when the circle was nearly complete, she seemed about to leap up and spring out, but that same expression of turmoil passed over her face again, and she sank to her knees. The Professor made a ring for himself too. His was to prevent a vampire from getting in. Mina's was to stop one from getting out.

Neither of them got much sleep that night. Mina had slept for most of the day, while the Professor was too scared, too cold, too racked with doubt to sleep. He had made a promise to Mina, the real Mina, the woman he had known and respected. And he had broken it. Only time would tell if it was the worst mistake he had ever made.

He was brought out of his contemplation by the sound of the horses. They were stamping at the ground. Then they began to whinny with fear, rearing up on their back legs, and before the Professor could do anything, they had snapped their ropes and bolted into the forest. At the edge of the trees, in a flurry of snowflakes, the Professor saw a great swirling shape begin to form. He shrank back, then glanced at Mina. The shape grew larger and more defined, then split into three figures. Although he had never seen them before, he recognized the figures only too well. They were the vampires that Jonathan had described in his journal. They were as terrible as he had thought with bright, cold eyes, sneering faces, and a chilling beauty.

"Mina!" the Professor shouted from within his circle, stretching his hands out to her.

"Do not fear for me," she said in a low, rasping voice. It was the first time she had spoken in days. "I am safe here. This is where I belong!"

As the Professor watched in horror, she threw back her head and laughed, the two long teeth glinting at each side of her mouth.

"Mina, resist this evil!" the Professor shouted, but Mina was no longer the Mina he knew.

"Come, sister," one of the vampires said softly. "Come to us, we are your friends!"

Mina moved closer to them, her arms outstretched. The vampires reached out to her. It seemed as though she would be enveloped in their arms.

"Mina!" he shouted once again.

Mina turned to him slowly.
"I'm thirsty!" she hissed.

The Professor felt his whole body shudder with disgust, but then, as Mina tried to step out of the ring, she gave an agonized shriek and was thrown back. It was as if some unseen force had picked her up and hurled her to the ground. She lay there whimpering, bewildered and dazed, as the three other vampires looked on.

"It was him," one of them snarled, pointing at the Professor with a long, pale arm. "He trapped her with – garlic," she spat, "and – Holy Water!"

With her two companions she began to advance upon the Professor.

"There won't be much blood in this old bag of bones!" the fair vampire said, laughing horribly.

The Professor shrank back, but then she too was thrown back when she tried to step into his circle.

The other two vampires hissed with anger, their fangs glistening. The Professor fumbled for his crucifix, then held it in front of him.

"Get back!" he commanded, raising himself from the ground, "get back to your foul lairs!"

The vampires moved away from him warily, powerless in the face of the cross. As they moved back into the forest they began to fade away, until finally they vanished completely. The Professor ran back to his circle and didn't stray from it again until daylight.

When he woke up after a few hours of uneasy rest, the Professor wasted no time. Leaving Mina in her circle, where he knew she would sleep all day, he set out for the castle. It took him over an hour to walk there. He shook his head in amazement at the height of the crumbling old walls. To think that Jonathan had climbed them! And there, in the courtyard, was the big door which had slowly creaked open, revealing Dracula. He wondered where the monster was now. Perhaps the others had already overtaken the boat and killed him. But perhaps not. . . Using a heavy hammer, the Professor forced the door open. Then, using Jonathan's journal as his guide, he searched for the chapel. He knew there were at least three coffins there, and he intended to find each one.

As he climbed down the spiral staircase that Jonathan had described, the air became putrid and rank, so he knew he was close. He entered the chapel cautiously, clinging tightly to the tools of his grisly task with one hand, and pressing a handkerchief to his nose with the other. He searched every nook and cranny, each room and chamber, determined to find Dracula's resting place. But when he finally stumbled into a dark, filthy vault it wasn't Dracula's grave he found. It belonged to the three vampires.

They lay in open coffins on the floor. The Professor stood over the fair-haired one. In her rest she was as beautiful as Lucy had been on that terrible night when Arthur had driven a stake through her heart. But then the Professor's eyes narrowed. This was no time for hesitation or doubt. Grasping the stake firmly in his hand, he placed its sharp tip over the vampire's heart.

As the hammer thudded down on the stake, a blood-curdling screech seemed to shake the castle to its very foundations. The body in the coffin shook and writhed. The Professor closed his eyes before he struck the stake a second time. When the shrieking stopped and all was still, he opened them again and stepped back in astonishment. In place of the body was just a small pile of dust. The vampire had crumbled away.

When he had dealt with the other two in the same way, he knew that he had rid the world of a great evil. But a greater evil still remained, and his next task was to destroy its sanctuary. Searching the rest of the chapel, he came across the crypt. It was a small chamber deep underground. Water dripped down the slimy stone walls and formed dirty, stinking pools on the uneven floor. The Professor had to step over them to get to the tomb in the middle of the room – a great casket, on a big stone plinth, the thousand-year old home of the most cunning and deadly vampire there had ever been. The one word carved into the plinth filled the Professor with dread:

DRACULA

The Professor opened the coffin and stared inside, thinking about the countless nights on which the monster must have taken refuge there, gorged with blood. Removing the stopper from his bottle of Holy Water, he slowly tipped its contents into the coffin. Dracula would never find sanctuary there again.

Back at the camp, Mina looked at him imploringly from inside her circle, almost as if she were trying to tell him something.

"What is it?" the Professor asked her quickly. "Tell me."

Mina seemed incapable of speech. She crouched on the ground with her head in her hands, as though engaged in a supreme struggle to conquer an unseen force.

"Go east. . ." she said finally.

"East!" Professor Van Helsing repeated with surprise. "If we go east we'll be going even farther into Transylvania, with no horses, few provisions, and no —"

"East. . ." Mina repeated, almost angrily.

The effort to speak at all, to resist the vampire in her, was now so great that she lost consciousness, sinking down into the snow. The Professor regarded her uneasily. In the night she had been a vampire, there was no doubt about that. Was it possible that she had managed to resist that evil force one last time so she could advise him where to go? And if so, why east? It was madness to go east. It was probably a trick, one of the cunning ploys that vampires use. The Professor knew what he ought to do – put this poor creature out of her misery, and head back west by himself. But. . .

The Professor went east. He didn't know why. It was something he couldn't explain even to himself as he helped Mina through the thick carpet of snow, always aware of her two sharp teeth near his neck. When she started to come to, he supported her with one hand, and kept a tight grip on his crucifix with the other. Never before had he felt so desperate or so lonely. The east-bound track seemed to wind on forever, with nothing certain at the end of it but his own death.

An hour or two before sunset, the exhausted Professor heard wolves howling. He couldn't see them, but he knew they were close and getting closer. He had to find somewhere safe to spend the night. Looking at the impenetrable trees on either side, he cursed himself for listening to Mina. But then the forest to the left petered out as the slope got steeper, becoming a crumbling rocky cliff over the valley below. Leaving Mina alone for a few minutes, the Professor clambered down and found a cave in the rock. It had a narrow entrance between two boulders, and was an ideal place to take refuge.

Some time later, contemplating death in the freezing cave, the Professor looked out over the Transylvanian valley. Far away he could see the huge range of the Carpathian mountains which pierced the sky like daggers. At the distant edge of the plain, a river snaked its way through the wilderness, twisting and curving into the middle of the valley where, half a mile away − suddenly the Professor jumped in surprise, banging his head on a rock.

"Mina! Mina, look!"

But Mina, lying motionless at the back of the cave, was incapable of looking. The Professor struggled to extract his binoculars from his bag. Thundering through the valley up to Castle Dracula was a group of mounted men. In their midst was a great wagon, pulled by eight horses and carrying a large box. The riders were swift and skilled, and looked very much like the gypsies Jonathan had described in his journal.

"My brave young friends have failed," the Professor whispered to himself in a halting voice. "They are probably dead."

Then he nearly dropped his binoculars. No wonder the gypsies were going so fast − behind them were three other horsemen! What they lacked in skill they made up for in guts and determination, and their horses were fairly flying over the snow-covered plain. It was Jonathan and the others. As the Professor watched, he could see that they were gradually catching up.

"Go on," he breathed, "go on!"

The wagon was on a course which would take it directly under the cliff. With his binoculars clamped to his eyes, the Professor saw Jack and Arthur, grim-faced and resolute, as they spurred their horses on and drew level with two fleeing gypsies. Shouting a quick word to each other, they leaped from their mounts onto the men. The four then tumbled to the ground, where the gypsies were quickly overpowered. The other gypsies slowed down in confusion. Their leader, a fiercesome looking man who was driving the wagon, issued a command. The wagon came to a halt, and the remaining horsemen surrounded it, each of them brandishing a weapon.

"Come on!" the Professor urged under his breath, glancing at his pocket watch. It was only a few minutes until sunset.

Arthur and Jack had now remounted and, led by Jonathan, were riding fearlessly at the gypsies. The look on their faces was so ferocious that, as they drew near, two of the gypsies suddenly panicked, broke away from the wagon and went galloping off. That left only five. They glanced nervously at each other, but held their ground.

Screaming like a banshee, Jonathan rode at them. Over his head he was swinging a huge wooden stake, and he knocked two of them clean over as he rode past, leaving them winded on the ground. He quickly wheeled his horse around. Jack and Arthur hadn't been very far behind, and they were engaged in one-to-one combat with the other gypsies. Jonathan dismounted and ran over to the wagon. The leader tried to block his path, but Jonathan couldn't be stopped. After a short struggle he pulled the man to the floor and held a pistol to his head. The man shouted a command to his followers. The battle was over. The gypsies surrendered, threw away their weapons and fled.

Letting go of the leader, Jonathan jumped onto the wagon. The Professor gasped at the sight of him. A wound in his stomach was bleeding, but he hardly seemed aware of it as he attacked the box. Arthur and Jack came to his aid, and between them, just as the sky began to darken, they wrestled the lid off.

There was Dracula, lying helpless in his coffin, but with that terrifying look of malevolence which they all knew only too well. For a split second, as the vampire saw the darkening sky, his red eyes flashed. It was only moments from sunset, when he would be able to change shape and escape. The Professor held his breath, expecting to see the monster transform into a huge wolf, or fade instantly into nothing. But this time there was no escape. The malevolent look turned to one of terror as Jonathan held a stake over his heart. Dracula frantically grasped it with both hands, but just as he did so Jonathan delivered a single mighty blow with a hammer.

Dracula didn't move, and made no sound. For several seconds his dying eyes glared in disbelief. Then, before Jonathan's triumphant gaze, the monster began to turn into liquid. The features on his face dissolved into a formless blob, which started to melt. Then his entire body oozed away, until there was nothing left of Dracula but a small, reeking pool of black sludge.

"We did it!" the Professor shouted triumphantly, turning to Mina, "we did it!"

"Did what?" Mina asked brightly, smiling at him as she woke up. Then she looked around at the cave. "Where am I?" she asked.

The Professor caught his breath as he looked at her. The hateful mark on her forehead had disappeared, and her vampire's teeth had gone.

"Back in the land of the living," was his reply.

It took them nearly an hour to clamber down the rockface. At the foot of the cliff, oblivious to the pain of his injury, Jonathan was waiting. Mina jumped from the last low rock, landing in the deep snow. Within seconds she was in his arms. They held each other tighter and tighter, speechless with relief.

Professor Van Helsing, still standing on the low rock, held out his lamp. He viewed the scene reflectively, then looked at Arthur and Jack holding the horses nearby. Jack put his arm around Arthur's shoulder, and he knew they were grieving for the woman they had loved. For a moment, the Professor closed his tired old eyes. He thought about Lucy, and how she died in Arthur's arms at Hillingham. He thought about the graveyard where they had seen her transformation. He thought about Carfax, where they had all but drowned in rats, and the house in Piccadilly where Dracula had eluded them. He thought about their desperate chase across the harsh landscapes of Transylvania to the very door of Dracula's castle. He contemplated wolves, bats, pain, suffering, fate and –

"Professor Van Helsing," Jack called, interrupting his meditations, "we owe you our thanks. We couldn't have defeated Dracula without you."

"We have all suffered so much," Arthur said quietly. "But without you we would have suffered even more."

"And I would have become a vampire," Mina said simply. The Professor sighed.

"We all played our part," he said. "I owe you my thanks for your courage and your endurance. We have had terrible moments, but we never gave up hope. That's why we succeeded. As for what you say, Mina, about becoming a vampire. . ." He paused, and his mind turned back to the dark deeds of the night, when she *had* been a vampire, when she had hissed those chilling words to him: *I'm thirsty*. . .

"Yes, Professor?" Mina asked. He hesitated, wondering how he could tell her. He looked at her and Jonathan, standing proudly together with their whole future ahead of them.

"I'm just more glad than I can say that you were spared that awful fate," he responded finally.

The truth was a secret he would take to his grave.

Other Versions of the Dracula Story

Dracula has been retold many times and it still inspires new versions in various forms, particularly films. Below are some examples of the best Dracula films, together with some other vampire tales too. All the films are readily available on video.

An early film version of the Dracula story was the silent *Nosferatu*, made in Germany in 1922 by F. W. Murnau. Though based on Stoker's novel, it does not follow the plot exactly, but it remains one of the most atmospheric films ever made. Tod Browning's *Dracula* (1931), starring Bela Lugosi, is the film that created the classic image of the vampire that most people think of today – a ghostly white figure in a formal dinner suit. It was the first in a long series of Dracula films made by Universal Studios in the 1930s, 1940s and 1950s. The original had dialogue, but very little music; in 1999 it was revived in a new version with music by the American composer Philip Glass.

Horror of Dracula (1958) was directed by Terence Fisher for the British company Hammer. An action-packed but quite accurate version of the Bram Stoker original, it starred Christopher Lee as Dracula and Peter Cushing as Dr. Van Helsing. The success of this film inspired Hammer to make many sequels.

Nosferatu (1979) was a remake by the German director Werner Herzog of Murmau's film of the same name. Starring Klaus Kinski as Dracula, it combines stunning photography with dark, brooding horror.

Bram Stoker's Dracula (1992), directed by Francis Ford Coppola, is probably Hollywood's most successful Dracula film. With a cast of stars that includes Keanu Reeves, Winona Ryder and Anthony Hopkins, and packed with special effects, it is a fairly faithful retelling of Stoker's novel.

Another Usborne Classic

FRANKENSTEIN

FROM THE STORY BY MARY SHELLEY

He made his way to the tank and peeped
over the rim. There was only the
smooth, undisturbed surface of the liquid
. . . Confused thoughts and troubled
emotions ran through his mind. He had
failed, it was true, but maybe that was
for the best. He sighed and relaxed
slightly. Then, from the liquid, a huge
hand shot out to grab him.

As lightning flashes across the night sky, Victor
Frankenstein succeeds in the ultimate scientific
experiment – the creation of life. But the being he
creates, though intelligent and sensitive, is so huge
and hideous that it is rejected by its creator, and by
everyone else who meets it. Soon, the lonely,
miserable monster turns on Victor and his family,
with terrifying and tragic results.